An END *of* SPEAKING

outskirts
press

BS
1174
.W2
2016

An End of Speaking
Stories of the Bible

Outskirts Press, Inc.
http://www.outskirtspress.com

ISBN: 978-1-4787-7897-4

Library of Congress Control Number: 2016912427

Outskirts Press and the "OP" logo are trademarks belonging to Outskirts Press, Inc.

PRINTED IN THE UNITED STATES OF AMERICA

To the Chabot
Library Folk!

> In woman's womb the word is made flesh.
> James Joyce, *Ulysses*

With love,

Joe

9/7/16

TABLE OF CONTENTS

REDACTOR'S NOTE BY M. CUSP

Zac spent 9 years writing these 9 stories and he has spent almost one year telling me that he didn't want anyone to read it anymore – that he did want that, but not anymore. Zac was also hot on his way into rehab for drugs. Two things are equally true: Zac does not do drugs anymore and he has no idea what he wants from this book I am forcing him to give to you.

He told me if this book is going to exist, I need to introduce it. *Do it calm and well and wise*, he says as those who know him know he says incessantly. Zac is an obsessive man. You either really will die for him or you really want him to die, for truths. I think readers will feel the same about this work.

The work, you must be willing to give up anything, even your job, for the Work. Zac looks happy often but never as happy when someone gets him talking about the Work. Zac also looks sad often, but less lately. Less since the clarity he worked so hard for. But he was 23 when he started this book that is coming out on his 33rd birthday. Zac loves 3 so much you would not believe it until you meet him. Then you will love 3 too. Or really hate it.

I think we only need to sell 100, M he tells me late one night. One of those late night calls when he pretends this book does not matter to him anymore. This is his first child. *It's hot, M, melting ice*. But other nights *its tired, M. Don't think it is saying anything fierce anymore*. If Zac consistently respects anything, it is ferocity.

I once went to a talk-thing he was doing and one of his colleagues who he always refers to as *my true secret sister* she said to the crowd, "Tonight you are going to experience what I experienced this semester teaching with Zac in Passion and Purpose – being around Zac can feel like a madman running through a zoo with all the keys – but every beast he lets out listens." And then Zac talked at our faces for 90 straight minutes. I am not convinced he breathed as much as he should have. And at the end, sweat drenched t-shirt, he says *and I didn't know this when I began but this was all for my mom and I love you mom you were so brave and if you do not hear one thing tonight hear this if you have ears to hear: life is not a line and we all will make enough money to die on time. Be kind no matter the cost. This is my great fire to offer you – you are already complete. Now all you need to do is become who you are.*

He smiled so big and the night ended and people were moved and he was happy. When we finished putting this book together for you, his smile was at least that large. I hope you enjoy this, or hate it. As my favorite Zac-ism would tell you: *NOTHING LUKE WARM!!!*

Because of Nik…

THE MAYOR

Then Cain went out from the presence of the Lord,
and settled in the land of Nod, east of Eden.

Genesis 4:16

Cain walked east toward nowhere. Toward Nod. Now on-
ward nowhere-bound for days, Cain could no longer smell
the lost bulbs of the Garden. His thirst had become a cloud, dry
and persistent as his shadow. He did not know where it was he
should be going. He wondered if he was being watched.

Over the ground were swooping dashes of grey. Cain looked
up into the sky but the sun was too bright. He had to close his
eyes. He opened them towards the dirt but instead of the soil all
he could make out were circles and worms of sun still left inside
of his head. He waited for them to pour out, but when they re-
mained he began to rub at his face, pleading at his eyes with his
fingers for his sight to return. His feet were little else but cracks
and dried blood. He needed water.

Cain thought of Eden. As boys he and his brother Able
would flock to the trumpet trees on hot days. Under their feet
was always a thick beard of grass. Cain thought to himself it was

the face of Yahweh's father and giggle, knowing that Yahweh had no father. It was grass. The two of them would race to the tree of hanging upturned blooms and together, with all their young strength, they would shake at the trunk until some of the trumpets would spill out the watery nectar. The boys would drink in the juice until their bellies felt as if they would burst, then they would chase each other about the trees with plump sticks, trying to get at the other to pop what had just been filled.

Now all Cain could see was dust. He felt at his water sack. He put his hand in a small pouch of seeds. How would anything grow, he wondered. Then he rubbed his brow with two fingers in a circular path. He walked on.

At night Cain could hear the restless grunts of beasts in the dark. It was too warm to make a fire, even when the sun had been absent for hours. Without sleep, Cain would sit and listen to the raucous breath of what he was told as a child was nothing, the unseen life outside of Eden that now he had been forced to learn. He could not say he missed his family, but in these moments when he was alone in the void of knowledge that was kept from him, he coveted the serpent's mind. What he would not promise if only the serpent was next to him in the night.

Dreams came quickly to Cain. He saw long fields of wheat and baskets of fruit. He saw the rain filling bowls and water overflowing the edges into two large hands. Then he heard rattles and crashes. Each drop of water had its own distinct shattering peal and then the hands would let the mass of water loose on a man, all of it, forming a ripe tomato red around the man. Cain woke and could not remember how or when the water had become blood. His heart thumped like the meeting of river and waterfall. He thought it was a dream that he would like to stop having.

Cain wondered if the serpent was accustomed to moving on his belly yet, and if perhaps he had grown to like it. Cain rubbed his brow.

In the morning the sun was bearable. Cain began to walk again, but not before he finished the necessary ritual of adding spit to the dust until a putty was made. This he would push into the sores of his feet. He remembered the first time his feet walked on something other than grass. His mother dragged him and Able through the Garden, as his father ran ahead. No one was chasing them. This was a new game the boys did not know. Once they were outside, Cain and Able saw Yahweh, but before they could run to him and clutch onto his massive arms to swing as they often loved to do, they were halted by his voice. Their parents fell to their knees and covered their ears. The boys stood short and waited. There, at that moment in time, for no reason at all it seemed to these two innocents, Yahweh changed their lives. He spoke the first woes they ever knew.

Cain continued to walk as the putty was melted by the sun. The removal of his only salve was remorseless. Cain thought of the soil. Yahweh had told the boys – as he looked straight ahead and above their eyes – that the soil would have to be worked. It was their curse. It was the consequence of their parents eating from Yahweh's tree. He had planted them a Garden and they were only to enjoy it, never to use it. Yahweh had wanted a Garden without necessity. He wanted to make humans to live in it without trying to become his equal – to simply exist in the splendor of the work of Yahweh's hand. He had made life but feared living. He had not thought everything through, Cain thought as a boy, as he stood listening to the awful words of his father's Father. He was confused and looked to his parents, but they were still on the ground locked together as if eating the other's end, quivering and crying. Able sat down. Cain walked closer to Yahweh, but Yahweh stepped back one giant step, longer than Cain's young legs could have traveled in an hour's sprint. But Yahweh's voice rang out. The soil must be worked and the Garden was no longer their home.

East had no meaning to Cain. It was simply away from the Garden. And it was the Garden alone that Cain cared for and missed. He needed to have that memory to continue walking away from it, as Yahweh had commanded him to do a few days before. Yahweh could force him to go, but he could not force him to forget that he had tasted of the tree as well. And that, Cain knew, is what Yahweh truly wanted.

*

Cain walked east for six days before he heard another voice.

"Come one, call all. Come one, you. You are all there is to come. Welcome, son. We have it all. Do not fear the Lord, here, son. We are the Lord. We have a code of our own."

Cain walked up to a large rock where a man in a tall hat stood. He was yelling to him even though he was so close. Cain had not seen a man for days. He wondered how he did not see the man until he was upon him.

"Who is the Lord?" Cain asked. The man began to laugh.

"The Lord, son? Oh, come on now. Don't go and kid me here in my own land. Sure, get me out where I might not know everything and sure, there you go on and kid me, son. The Lord. The one who put that nasty smudge in your head."

Cain had almost forgotten the mark.

"You can tell me. No harm there. Here, in fact, you can tell me anything. Might as well, son. I already know. Now go on, give me the tale. What did you go and do that got the Lord so upset that he went and tossed you out on your hind-end? Go on, I love these stories."

Cain could not speak. It was as if the man's voice had made him mute. He desperately wanted to speak, to tell this round and thunderous man everything he knew and ask him everything he wanted to know, but he had no words.

The man walked down from the stage and took off his hat to reveal a thick patch of hair colored by the midday glow of shadeless heat, waving back and forth like the blurred vision of a mirage.

"I can see you have walked a long way, son. Here, why don't you and I go on and get out of this open air and see if we can't get a nice conversation started, for starters." The man laughed again. "Here, take my hand and give it a good shake. That's how we do things here. Go on, grab it firm and give it a shake."

"Where am I?" Cain asked.

"You are in Nod, son."

"Who are you?" Cain sputtered.

"I am the Mayor of this fine city, Cain. I heard you might be coming."

*

Cain opened his eyes to an eclipse. The Mayor's giant head was blocking out the sun, crouching just behind the expanses of his hair and ears. It was like a new hat, radiant and temporary.

"There's a good boy. Open up and yawn it out, son. Rattle out those webs, now. Up you are. Get up, Cain." The Mayor grabbed Cain under each arm and hoisted him from the dirt towards the sky. Once his feet were planted the Mayor gave him a rigorous dusting.

"I was asleep," Cain said.

"More like you turned off for an hour or so," the Mayor laughed. "Too much to take in, perhaps. Seems you were not expecting me as I was you?"

"Expecting. No. No, I was not. I was thirsty."

"Sure, sure. I knew that. Come now. Let's get inside and get on with the refreshing."

The Mayor walked Cain away from the rock. In the near distance Cain could see dwellings, and in a few minutes they grew into a sight unlike anything Cain had ever seen in or out of the Garden. It was a forest of human-craftsmanship. The things that grew were outnumbered by the things that were made.

"What do you say, son? Here she is. Nod. Our city. Your city."

"City, sir?"

"I keep forgetting, Cain. You need to be caught up. City, son, is what we call the places we build to stave off the wild. City is home. City is family. And you are quite welcome, too." T h e Mayor put one of his thick hands on Cain's neck and squeezed, trying to make the man know he was truly not alone. The Mayor loved beginnings.

Cain feared family. The Mayor could see it in the poor man's eyes. The slackness of his shoulders at the sound of the word.

"In here, Cain, is where our day will begin. Time to irrigate that throat of yours and get your feet into some rest."

The Mayor led Cain into a large tent where inside the space smelled of cooked meat and heat-ruined fruit. The energy in the place swirled with guffaw. Cain knew nothing of what he saw or felt. He tried to keep himself from looking behind him. He tried not to be afraid. His fingers and brow were sore.

The two men sat down at a table and as soon as their feet touched the floor a foam spewing barrel was set down in front of them. Cain looked up at the woman and his shoulders immediately found filling.

"Feels good to sit, eh son? Here, let me pour you a glass. You must be very parched. Me too, I must say. Every morning! We call this The Grease of the Vine. Have a drink."

Cain took a deep draught. "Sir, I think this *grease* has gone bad."

"No, son. It has gone good." He called at the woman. "Send for Bata and tell him to bring a glass. Tell him the wheels need greasing!" His wide and happy laugh seemed to push her from the table.

"Okay, Cain. Ask me anything. Tell me something. Time to talk."

Cain took another drink. "My feet tingle."

"I almost forgot about those. Here, let me find something for you to wrap your wounds in."

"No, sir. They tingle. They feel better. I had to walk a long way in pain. Now they tingle."

"Yes, your walk was long. Nod is a long way from the Garden. Tell me, Cain. Why were you sent to me? Why did Yahweh cast you away from your father and mother and brother?"

Cain was silent behind his glass. His mind began to hiss. The tingling of his feet was now in his ears.

"Cain, son, I don't believe in exile. I believe in speaking. I believe in the power of a full glass and an honest afternoon. You did wrong by Yahweh. That does not mean he did not do wrong by you. But I need to know. Why are you marked?"

"How do you know all of this?"

*

That day Cain felt the curse stronger than was usual. He had been in the fields before the sun and his work was heavy on his back. The ground was yielding, but not at his will. It was force and persistence that pulled from the seed what he wanted. Able sat under a tree watching the flock.

It was almost time to feel the shade of day's end when the two young men heard Yahweh call for them. He wanted to see the best of how they filled their days. He wanted to see the fruit of their labors. It was time they validated the hope in his creation that Yahweh had cultivated after the sins of their parents.

Able led to Yahweh a fat, bright lamb. Cain carried a basket of golden wheat.

Yahweh regarded the two offerings for but a moment.

"I am pleased with the lamb. I am not pleased with the wheat."

Cain was incensed at how arbitrary these words seemed to him. "Yahweh, can you tell me what is wrong with my offering? Can you tell me why you are not pleased with what I have worked from the soil?"

"Why are you angry, Cain? Why has your countenance fallen?"

"Why am I angry! I spend more hours with the soil than the Sun! You are always watching. I know you are! You see the work of my hands. You set me to be the one to work the curse of the ground and gave Able the flock and I have done it and done it well. You see what I grow for our family! The flock lives on its own. Who is there for him to be watchful? And yet you watch me and see my work. My countenance? Fallen! What else would you have me bring you?"

Yahweh held the heavy basket of wheat at the end of his last finger and inspected it. Then he looked into Cain. "If you do well, will not your countenance be lifted up? And if you do not do well, sin is crouching at the door; and its desire is for you, but you must master it."

"What are you speaking about? Sin? I have done the work you charged me with. You can see my sweat. All I have done is what you told me I must. I have toiled in silence under your watch! What else must I do? You speak of sin? Speak to me of what is good."

"I am not pleased with the wheat. I am pleased with the lamb."

*

"You must remember, Cain, that Yahweh was the first planter," the Mayor said.

"None of this was Able's fault, sir. But I could not take the knife to Yahweh. Able was there. That is all."

"Cain, you did wrong by your brother, but one thing I have learned, son, is that wrong does not always outgrow good. You still have years to till, son. Years to till."

The two men sat at the table with the still foaming barrel between them.

"One thing you have to realize in Nod, son, is that the one sin that is not tolerated is the sin of Yahweh. You have to be willing to forget about yourself some, son. The world will never revolve right around you."

"He cast me out. I can never forget that."

"Sure, sure. No one is telling you that you need to forget. But you also need to remember, son, that you are not the first to be banished, and knowing old Yahweh like I do, you will not be the last."

"You *know* Yahweh?"

"Like a brother, son. He would never say that but it is true. You miss the fullness of the Garden. I miss its youth. I can still feel the seeds in my hand when I dream."

"What are you saying?" Cain feared he would wake again without knowing he had fallen asleep. He focused hard on keeping awake to the words being spoken.

"Son, you don't really think Yahweh did all that work of the Garden alone, do you?"

"Yes, sir, I do. Or did. Sir, you must realize that until I met you I thought I was banished from the only people in the world."

"Don't be a fool, son. If that was true, then why would Yahweh have marked you? Who would he be protecting you from? If you and your family was all there was, how would Yahweh expect you to multiply? Come on, son, you must fill in the gaps. Here, let me tell you a story."

"Can I have some more Grease first?"

The Mayor filled both glasses and settled into his chair.

"Yahweh is not one for competition, son. Never was and never will be. We spent many days together in the chaos. The Void. Those were strange times, son. Elohim was ready for order, and we were in charge of making it. So we started to plant. Yahweh was given authority to set things up as he thought best, and that was fine by me. Not everyone liked the choice, but that is really an entirely different story for a different time, I'd say. So we planted. Some went off their own way, but I stuck by Yahweh and we worked."

The Mayor's eyes had rain on the horizon.

"It was good work to do, son. Our planting was going to balance out chaos. It was important work. But Yahweh did not want balance. He wanted eradication. He thought the Garden should choke out chaos, you see. He overplanted."

At this point of the story another man walked up to the table. His beard had grey enough to be twice the age of Cain. He smiled as if he had just been very close to a woman. The Mayor stood up and took the man's hand in his.

"Bata! Good, good. Finally. Seems like I called for you hours ago! Cain, this is my good friend Bata. He has been living in Nod for some time now. I think you two will like each other very much. You have similar stories."

Cain put out his hand towards Bata. Bata shook it with care. It was new to Cain, after all.

"Okay, so where was I. Bata, have a large drink. You have heard this one before. So, back to Yahweh. He truly wanted to make the Garden a place without chaos. Without choice. It was a bad idea, of course. But Elohim had given him the power and for a long while I worked under his watch, unsure of what else I could do. Then came the serpent."

The serpent. Cain had almost forgotten the great curiosity of his childhood. The serpent.

"One day I was on the western rim of the Garden, lolling about, taking in some heat, when I heard a rustling. Out of the thrush walked the serpent, smiling, as always. He came near to me, wary, and simply said, 'Yahweh's will is dangerous. You know the space chaos gives us. The Garden is growing too fast.' And I knew he was right, sure I did, and I told this all to Yahweh."

"What did he say?" Cain asked.

"He said he had it all under control. That he would make Man. That Man would tend to the Garden and help keep chaos away. The Void would be forever filled. Man would sustain his power over it."

"And the serpent?"

"Well, the serpent held the seeds of chaos. He said they must be planted. For the sake of Man, he said, we must plant them. He said it was wrong of Yahweh to create Man and not allow them to know what they were missing. He said it was up to us."

Cain could almost taste the fruit of the Tree now. He hoped the Mayor still had some of the seed.

"So we did. Behind Yahweh's back we planted the seed and the Tree grew. It held the life Yahweh feared. So I was banished, forever, from the Garden I had helped grow. So I grew Nod. And that's that, son. I was the first Mayor of Nod and I will be the last Mayor of Nod."

The Mayor took a proud sip and wiped his pink mouth from west to east.

"And why did Yahweh not banish the serpent, sir?" Cain's mouth and mind had tangled themselves together. He had ceased to wonder what should be believed.

"Oh, he did, son. But you know the serpent. He knows too much. He finds ways around such things. And it drives Yahweh mad.

And that leads me to where I was going with all of this, Cain. You don't go and feel too bad. It is envy that turned Yahweh's regard away your wheat, see? It is *because* you did well that he would not accept your work. But all is well. In Nod, we respect the work of a good planter. Right , Bata?"

*

It was a morning in the Garden where every color insisted on being splendid long past the dawn. Cain's mother and father had left the boys alone, as they often did, in order to further understand the things they did that made new life. The boys used this time to wander, finding each time that the Garden was transformed, but without understanding of how – how the plants seemed to bring to each day a fresh idea of how to grow.

Cain decided they should follow the reds, that their romp should be directed by following the most distinctive reds in view. They reached a narrowing of the river when Cain saw a flash of maroon in the corner of his vision. He ran after it, but quickly Able was upon him, holding him to the ground. Able knew the way to the Tree was close. Cain could not follow the flash.

As the boys wrestled over the right for decision, the boyhood struggle in the dirt and grass that would continue long past their fears and death, there was a heavy, yet nimble scampering heard behind their coiled limbs. It was the one beast their father never named. The one who came named already.

"Boys. It is time we speak."

Able unhooked himself from his brother and went running in the direction of his parents. Cain did not follow Able with his legs or eyes or heart. He had dreamt of this moment and never knew why or how he could confess until now. The serpent. The Guardian of the Forbidden Tree. The one, his parents told him often, that Yahweh did not love.

12 AN END OF SPEAKING

"You stay and will speak?" the serpent asked.

Cain trembled.

"Yahweh says you are not his," Cain said.

"Yahweh has never spoken of me to you, has he, son? These are the words of your parents, are they not?"

"They are. They say Yahweh says you are not his."

"Well, I am not. I am my own. As you are your own, and as your mother and father are their own. Even as Able, your swift brother, is his own."

"I do not understand. Yahweh made us. We are his."

"Yes, yes. Yahweh made you. From the ground. And the ground is not Yahweh's. He did not create out of nothing or even out of himself. He created out of the chaos, son. And chaos is not his. None of this is Yahweh's. He must make it so in Seem, not Being."

"I am a boy. I am Yahweh's boy and my mother and father's boy. I do not understand your words."

"No, not yet, son. But here. Will you walk with me? It is one of the great joys to walk in the Garden when it grows to the West against the grain of the Sun."

"I will."

The serpent walked next to Cain with his slender hand on his neck. They walked through the river together where two great folds of the Garden's canopy fluttered open for a moment, coaxing a gush of sun to guide them back to the far side of the bank.

"What do you know of the Tree, son?"

"That it is not to be eaten of. That if we eat of its fruit, we will surely die."

"Tell me, Cain. What is this death?"

"I do not know."

"What do they tell you the Tree is called, Cain?"

The young boy stretched his mind taunt around the question.

He did not, somehow, want to disappoint the serpent by answering with the wrong words.

"It is called the Tree of the Knowledge of Good and Evil."

"Yes, yes. I have heard that name as well. Tell me, then, what is Knowledge? What is Good? What is Evil?" The serpent made his hand more apparent on the boy's skin.

Cain had never been asked these questions before. Never asked them of himself and this filled his mind with an unknown ruckus that scared away the peaceful order of the setting sun and rising moon – filled him with a sense of pity for his parents that he did not want to hold as you do not hold the middle of fire – filled him with what he would later know as heaviness – filled him with the silence of falling leaves.

"I do not know, serpent. I do not know what to call anything. Or why anything is called something. I do not know."

"Ah, there it is." The Tree stood there before the two and the serpent took his hand off of the boy with a slight push. "This is the Tree, Cain."

Cain looked at the Tree with empty wonder. This was what could end his life. What Yahweh hated. What his parents spoke more about than love. This was the Tree that could end all the games. And it was but a Tree. Not the tallest or the shortest, the fattest or the slimmest. It was a Tree. He did not understand.

"Cain, I do not want to confuse you. May I speak simply?"

"Please, serpent, please simply, please."

"Yahweh has great power. He is mighty. He is not only Evil, a word to be feared if you do not understand it. But he is not only Good, a word to be cautious about even if you do understand it. He is young in his power, and he can still be both Good and Evil. But he does not know this. Because of his power, he thinks he can only be Good. And that is why we need this Tree. You and your family – you do not have Knowledge. You do not know of

Good and Evil and Yahweh wants this because then Yahweh cannot be questioned. Do you understand my words, son?"

Cain did not know if he did. He was also young, he thought. He did not know what he was capable of, or how to question.

"I do not know, serpent."

"Would you like to know?"

"Yes, serpent, but I am afraid to know."

"Then you are ready to eat."

*

"Bata, my good friend. What do you say we get some food in us. Too much Grease without some Fat and this city would wash away. Cain, you have never eaten like you will in Nod."

"I am hungry, sir. My stomach now tingles."

"Yes, yes. I am sure it does, son. We can fix that. We know how to eat in Nod, right Bata?"

Bata smiled a lengthy, riveted smile at Cain. "Yes, Cain, my new friend. We can put down the Fat in Nod. Best around."

"Can you tell me about yourself while we wait for the Fat?" Cain asked Bata.

"I can. But I think the Mayor tells the story better. He has told it more times than I have."

Cain looked to the Mayor for an answer, but the Mayor's face was hidden behind his glass.

"What? Oh, sure sure. I can tell Bata's tale, too. But let's make it quick. Cain can only take so much in one day, right son?"

"Yes, sir. But after my walk, Grease and tales are not difficult to take. I feel familiar here. I like this. You have a pleasant voice for stories."

"Well, Cain, Bata here had a rough go of things way back. He comes from the South, whereas you come from the West. But Bata had some troubles with his brother, too. And his Yahweh, so to speak, was not much help in the matter, either."

The Mayor filled the three glasses. He wanted things filled.

"Bata was the younger brother. His older brother, Anubis, owned him. Bata would spend the day working the fields and tending the livestock, doing the work of two men. All this work made Bata the strong bull you see before you, now even many years later. Anubis had a wife that wanted this bull, you see, and she threw herself at him one day while he was working. Imagine, Cain, if that woman who brings us the Grease threw herself at you, what would you do?"

Cain was silent. He drank.

"I do not know. If it was Able's woman I would not."

"Well, neither did Bata. He denied his brother's wife, but the woman, furious at being denied by a dumb bull, told Anubis that his brother had tried to force himself on her. Bata cried out to Ra, his Yahweh, but Ra did not set things straight between the three. So to prove his innocence, our good friend Bata had to cut off his penis to prove he was pure. Imagine his countenance, eh!"

Cain spit some of his drink. "What? What happened?"

"The penis fell. What was it, Bata, again? Eaten by what now?" the Mayor loved this ending.

"Catfish. Eaten by a catfish."

"Aha, yes! A catfish of all things. So ever since I heard Bata's tale I have forbidden the eating of penis and fish in Nod." The Mayor held up his glass to Bata. "As any good Mayor would do."

"Why didn't Ra save you from all of this?" Cain asked. "You did nothing wrong. Do you still serve Ra?"

Bata lost his smile and looked at Cain with the calm of a meadow after thunder. The Mayor set his glass down.

"Serve Ra, son?" the Mayor said. "Bata lives in Nod, now. There is no room for Ra. Do you understand my words?"

*

The Mayor carried Cain over his shoulders like a fresh kill. His gate tumbled some, under the weight of the young man, and his mind rolled with Grease and disappointment. He wanted this day to be more.

"Poor boy," he mumbled. "Fat came too late for him. Too much vine, I suppose. I should have known better." He readjusted his burden. "Well, tomorrow is a new day for the boy. Tomorrow. But for now." His thoughts trailed off as the wind tried to make Cain into a sail. The Mayor focused on the task of getting his new citizen to bed.

On the way to the center of town the Mayor caught site of one of his favorite dwellings. It was a large wood framed tent, large enough for an army of war elephants.

"Aha, the Men of Renown!" the Mayor gruffed. "I forgot to tell Cain about the Men of Renown. Now that is a Tale to be Told! Tomorrow. A fresh morning. More stories. Less Grease. But tonight, more, more, I'd say. But not for Cain. Tonight and bed."

The Mayor was unaware of the tumbleweeds in his memory at this moment. They were held at bay by the precious breathing weight he now had charge over.

He reached his home at the North end of the city. He lay Cain down in the front room softly so as not to arrest his dreams. "Cain, this will be a new sleep for you. It will be slumber and you will know it in full. I decree." He laughed at his speech. It sounded to him out of his mouth like nothing he had in his head. His head had grown raucous, but his unheard words were without ripple. "I like this boy. Needs get a new language, but good. Get him in the fields soon where he belongs. Work and laugh. Need to sweat the curse out."

Once he felt Cain was comfortable, the Mayor wandered about his home with an ether step, flowing, jubilant, and awed at the power that resided in his ambitions. He searched for his favorite skin.

"Some white to go with all the red," he said to himself as he poured from the skin a full bowl and brought it to his mouth. "Time to sit and sift," he thought or said. It did not matter now that night had taken over.

In his den, he walked about and brushed the gaggle of hanging chimes hung about with his strong free hand. It was creation to make them clack and spin. He pitied the serpent, for now that he was forced to crawl, he would never be able to clack a chime and feel this large. It was a joy he desperately wanted to share with his old brother of the Garden. He thought of Yahweh.

"Yahweh would not appreciate a good chime. No, no, not for one moment. With a chime, you see," he laughed at his speech again, wondering who he addressed, "with a chime you never know what sounds might spring forth. That is it. No controlling a chime. And with a chime the wind can also control. Chimes are chaotic, you see. Yes. Chaotic, but beautiful. Necessary."

He sat down as if falling, yet managed to keep every drop in the bowl. The room resounded. Pleasant gongs and whistles. Chirps of wood. Birds of song made by the man sitting and listening. Created by the Mayor. This made him proud and awake in his recollections. He was very friendly with these sounds and trusted the next noises they might make. He drank from the bowl, the liquid only held back by his grin.

The Mayor thought of what he had accomplished and how he had failed. How he never could have known he would be in charge of the misfits of arbitrary divine decree. The results of young gods with great power. He did not pity Yahweh or his counterparts. His pity was reserved for the refuse, like the young man asleep in his home and like the old man Bata with his flattened front. He thought of his citizens and wanted to throw a party. Tomorrow, tomorrow was for plans. Tonight, the night was for the mind to dig and forage. Too see anew in the dark and adjust to what the day had offered.

"Yahweh is forever to miss it," he said. "Missing this, this, well, community. Communal community. The serpent, too, will miss it. They want the same thing, I see. To keep out the night. Yes, the night and the darkness. Yes, that is what they want. Or, perhaps, the serpent wanted the Tree to illuminate everything, for all to be in the light. But no, no, for that too, is a sort of darkness. Too much. Both want too much. Yahweh wants the darkness in the minds of his creation, his jealousy for the Known, and the serpent to fill the creation for the Want of the Known. Yes, both want the same thing in opposite directions, you see. But soon they will have to Touch!"

The Mayor was drunk. The bowl needed to be filled. His mind was shrinking now into disordered emotion and he drank from the bowl to hold it back or to let it flow, he did not know which. He thought of all he could tell and show Cain tomorrow. All he had made grow. Then he thought of his own youth and what had been harvested from his hands. It quickly became too great for his night to hold. He could feel a rush of seeds gathering behind his eyes and he did not want them to drown this night, not until he understood them, so he closed his eyes and held back a sea.

An End of Speaking

The place you are standing borders the holy.

Exodus 3:5

I never thought I would write about him or us, or really anything that has taken place over the last forty years. I never thought he would leave me. But looking back as I'm forced to now, old and alone, I should have expected this pain. Yahweh did it to so many.

This rock feels far away from Midian. I want to say *home*, but I have always been a man without that. I was born a Jew, the son of two slaves living in a foreign land. For three months I had a home with them, but soon I had to trade in the bed of my mother's arms for a crib of papyrus. And soon the Nile would be my land. I wonder now if he was watching me then, guiding that basket bed along the banks. So powerful, those two forces – the river of the Gods and the one who decides when he wants to be God, and when he wants to be gone. As far as I know he was absent then on my trip from my parent's poverty into the house of God on earth. But he may have been walking along in the reeds, watching my infant face shift between bliss or confusion,

sleep or fear – and who is to say how any of that would make him feel. Who's to say a butterfly may not have flown by and distracted him from observing the future leader of his people capsizing? There are many things I'll never know, especially now as he has told me my time is short. I only wish I knew when he really chose me. And why.

I gave up my life for him but it was never enough. The Jealous One, Jealous Yahweh – his favorite self referential phrase – always needed more.

There is no place to begin that I will feel right about. That is why I write at all now, because I know I will never feel right again. My life is over and I am a man without validation. All the people that left Egypt under my guidance are long dead. The people he is leading into the Promised Land now never tasted slavery and neither did I, come to think of it – really depends on how you understand my service to him the last four decades. Although, I was there when my people suffered at the hands of the slave drivers. I heard their cries. I saw the blood, the broken bones. The one man with the rib jutting through his old skin out his side in the mud like a piece of brick straw. And then one day it became too much for me to bear. I defended a Jew and became a murderer. Then an exile, a shepherd, a husband, a father, a visionary, a revolutionary, a leader hated and loved, and now a patsy, a victim, a lunatic. But when do those transitions take place?

"Who am I?" It was all I could think to say when he first spoke to me from the bush of flames. I told him from the beginning that I was not a man of words, not a man who has control over my speech. But he was asking me to be his voice to Pharaoh. There was no reason why he could not go to the Pharaoh himself, unless he was scared too. He only talked to me, everything else was mediated through my mouth or his impetuous actions.

His whims. "Go to Pharaoh," he says. "Tell him he will let my people Israel go." His people. He reminded me of this constantly, as if I was questioning him. They didn't even know him. He was the God of the Hebrews in his mind only, but that was enough for me. How did he not see I was obedient from the start? Why did he think he had to prove his power – the persuasive energy that poured from him? Why did he have to put the innocent Egyptians through ten plagues, why did he force his people to suffer all those forty years in the desert, why won't he let me go in? His words are burned in me – the last words I will ever hear him speak.

"This is the land I vowed to Abram, to Isaac, and Jacob. To your seed I will give it. That was my promise to you. It is revealed to your eyes though your body cannot follow."

Never hear the tumult of his voice again. The crashing of his pathologies. I want to be with him. I deserved the land. I made all of this possible. I kept his people from deserting him. I kept him from killing off the entire nation more than once. He asked of me more than was fair and I gladly gave it. I kept him sane through his experiments and now the best he can do is tell me once I die he will bury me. He is a master of forgetting these promises. No doubt I will rot at this rock. Ravens. All about.

In the early days I was confident in him. I knew he would be something great, something to be written of for centuries. I was blessed to be his right hand man. Watching the way he toyed with the Pharaoh was numbing in its grandeur.

"Moses. He will let them go and I will have you lead them into a land of promise. A rich land. A land of plenty and ease. Nations will fall before my people and you will be mine. Like the sand on the shore shall be your seed." It wasn't rare to catch a glimmer of self-satisfaction on his face when he spoke like this. He made you tremble with the discomfort of greatness. And he wanted me.

Zipporah was jealous of my place with Yahweh. My wife never trusted him. After he told me I was to go to Egypt to free the Jews she swore he tried to kill me in my sleep. I know this cannot be. I asked him many times to kill me when the weight of his needs was too much. But he ignored me in these moments. Could be he never heard my words unless they were repeating back his words. But she claimed until her last breath that he came to our tent that night while I was asleep with hate and blood in his eyes. Her story makes no sense – circumcising our son and throwing his foreskin on me, telling Yahweh, "Moses is a bride-groom of blood to me." This, she claims, caused Yahweh to go away. Can't be. If he had wanted to kill me he would have had no trouble. Countless thousands died by his hand during my life with him. Egyptian babies, thousands of Egyptian babies died as the punctuation mark to the end of his sentence on Pharaoh.

He was so pleased with himself as he laid out the plan to me.

"In the middle of the night I will appear in the midst of Egypt. And he will die – each first one in Egypt, from the son of the Pharaoh who sits on the throne to the son of the slave maid sitting behind the millstone – to every beast firstling. There will be a great screaming throughout Egypt – as never before, nor ever to be. I will not hold back the Slaughterer, who enters to deal death wherever he goes."

I never asked him if he saw the irony in any of this. Certainly I would not have ended up in Pharaoh's house had it not been for a similar decree made against all the first born of Israel. I was saved from that murderous edict. None of the children of Egypt were so lucky. Yahweh, if nothing else, was always efficient and thorough. When it was finished he came back to me, desperate it seemed to tell me the news.

"Pharaoh awoke in the night – he and his officers, all Egypt – to a great scream: there is no house where there is not a dead man."

Panting, he ran through the killings as if it was being read off the parchment of his mind's eye. I was troubled, but also very impressed. The God of the Hebrews, my Yahweh, was the most powerful thing on the earth.

The people doubted him, of course, but I was convinced he knew exactly what he was doing.

"Do not be afraid," I would tell them incessantly, "You will see the freedom Yahweh is creating. Yahweh is fighting for our futures."

Those words mean nothing now. We are all dead. Soon. Soon I will join them in Sheol. If he loved me like I always hoped he did he would have killed me instead of leaving me to look out over my pain's expanse. He would have taken my memories. He would have let me sleep one night in Canaan. He would slick my thirst with something other than this skin of wine he left with me. Tradition tells us that Noah, once brought through the flood, planted a vineyard and got quite drunk off of his first harvest. So drunk he was found naked in his tent by a son. But Yahweh did not give me enough wine to get drunk with. He could have at least done that.

I remember a time when he allowed me no food or drink for forty days. He called me up to Mt. Sinai, the place that became his refuge during our time in the desert. He was working out the covenant he wanted to strike with us. This was hard for him. He was much better suited to order and react, and this sort of attempt at community with the people was dizzying. It was strange and terribly vivid to watch him during this time. He told me I was not to eat or drink or speak until he said I could. I starved and withered but he would sometimes come near me and his emanation, his brilliance sustained me. He would mumble to himself. The Garden and the Snake. I could never make out anything complete. I imagine he was questioning kicking them

out of paradise and I can only hope he will question never letting me see it. Knowing him, I will die before he admits this mistake.

I have to accept that it was my mistake that made him leave me here. I, of all people, know how important his words are to him. Not to follow every syllable was the crazy act of an old fool. I had survived questioning his words before, but barely. The people were grumbling about the manna Yahweh was feeding us all with.

"In Egypt we had pots of flesh," they called out, "Why has Yahweh taken us out of Egypt to die of bread in this wilderness?"

I brought this concern to him, I myself thinking meat was not a wrong request. Not surprisingly, he was offended. His reaction – "Is the arm of Yahweh too short? I will give them more meat than they could possibly eat in a year. Soon you and your people will see what becomes of my words!" It was interesting to listen to when they were *my* people and when they were *his* people. I would not have survived calling them my people. And his word was true. Quail filled the horizon. Sick, dreadful, maggot stuffed quail. He didn't speak to us for weeks while we dealt with the meat.

I saved this people from his crazed caprice. I gave up my own fortune for them. They were never assured that this Yahweh I told them so much about was going to bring them into any Promised Land. Often they called to be brought back to Egypt. When he heard this he went mad.

"How long will this people affront me? How long until they attend to me, and see the signs I put before them? Why is it you cannot make them see me as I am to be seen? I will put a disease in front of them and erase their inheritance. I will make a nation out of you alone, grander then they, enormous. I will bring you into the Promise to thrive. They are dead as I speak."

I made the choice to fight for them as I had told them he

was doing all along. "If you kill off this people, the people you rescued, the entire world will say that Yahweh is not capable of sustaining his people. He took them out of slavery simply to die in the desert. You will be a mockery. Your people will repent of their complaining if you allow them to. Soften their hearts just as you hardened Pharaoh's."

"The children I will allow to grow while I make carcasses out of the men and women who complained. You will bring the younger generation into the land."

I must have been old in my mind even as a young man to pass up his offer to make the nation out of me. I did not know this would happen. Slow madness and death limping to me across the sand as the wind blows the strings of my wine skin. He has to come back for me.

He took my staff. The staff he gave me when we first met. The staff he allowed me to do great miracles with in the house of Pharaoh. The staff that was my only real companion as I aged in the desert trying to keep afloat in the chaos of his newly born destinies. As a younger man I used this staff to bring water to the people.

"Yahweh, the people are thirsty. They have had no water for days."

"Go and strike that rock with your staff and you will see fresh water flowing for my people."

And now, just a few days ago, or however long it has been, the staff betrayed me. I betrayed him with the staff. The people were thirsty again and he told me, "Go speak to this rock and it will bring forth water."

I don't know why I struck the rock again. His words said 'speak' and I struck. Then his words said, "You will not enter the land. You have not heeded my words. You will die with the wandering generation, outside. Call Joshua to the tent of meeting. He will lead his generation."

Then, as if all he needed was an excuse to let me go, we came to the land. Forty years of this desert, forty years of Yahweh and now he shows me the land I cannot have. It was spectacular – from Gilead to Dan, all of Naphtali, the land of Ephraim and Manasseh, and all the land of Judah out to the Western Sea, all the Negev, past the oasis palms of Jericho, and throughout all the valley of Zoar. All for Joshua.

He always told me he would be in the minds of men for the rest of creation. I never cared about that. I cared for my time with him. Now all there is is my mind. Even the wine is gone. I don't have the strength to remember anymore and what of it can be trusted. Who am I to say.

* note: portions of Yahweh's dialogue are adaptations or ap-propriations of David Rosenberg's translation of the original Hebrew from the book of Exodus in *The Book of J* by Harold Bloom. New York: Vintage Books. 1990.

Down that Ashen Road

What kind of man was he who came up to meet you
and spoke these words to you?

2 Kings 1:7

My mother once, more than once, told me I would regret every decision I made once I left the Way. I know nothing of what Province you may come from, or if you might know anything of the Way, but I can almost be certain it is nothing like what you think. It is a no-thing. There is no way to tell you, in kindness, no way you will understand.

The Way is unspeakable. Something to be followed or searched after, a thing once near as thunder in your ears and soon silent as drying dew. The Way has led many men to do many things. It is why mothers tend to be more sympathetic of devotion to the Way, because all mothers want their sons to be remembered, at any cost.

Even if you are not from our people, or a nearby land, you surely know of our great men who have followed the Way. Slaves have been freed, a nation begun, Judges appointed and Kings crowned. Wise men and prophets and brave warriors.

Giants felled and entire peoples laid waste. Some have been lifted up. But no story is so simple. No truth so flat. No history so clean. Especially when you, as I, deal with the dead. Once you care to your first body you know, with the immediacy of sight, that the Way is not a *the* but an *a*.

*

I lived in a time where few men held awful power. I still do. I am no expert when it comes to this matter, what some have taken to call The Story, but it seems to be, at least on the cursory level that my mind can operate, that all times have been like our own. Who decides these things, I ask, while knowing what is called the answer all too well. My job allows me the space to muse, however, on the nature of power and breath and this reality referred to as life.

The dead being great teachers of time.

We are taught to worship the idea of the dead by men who never touch the dead, men who, out of ignorance that is called leadership, never have to wrestle with the unwanted textures of living. The first leader of the Way was not like this. If he were alive, I suspect, I would not be who I am.

We are also taught that the actual dead bodies that litter our grounds are unclean and to be despised. Perhaps they remind us to much of Sheol, those vast leveling grounds on the far banks of our knowledge, that meeting place between what is felt in our hands and what tumbles down from the mountains of our minds. What we know and what we do not. Perhaps when our leaders see or even think of the dead they are repulsed by the possibility that they are only men. That one day another man will lay them down.

*

Go down at once, for your people, whom you have brought up out of Egypt, have corrupted themselves. They have turned quickly aside from the Way which I commanded them. I have seen this people and they are an obstinate people. Now let me alone, that my anger may burn against them, that I may destroy them; and I will make of you a great nation.

I will be gracious to whom I will be gracious, and I will show compassion to whom I will show compassion. You cannot see my face! No mere man can behold my face and live! I will pass before you, but you may only see my back. You shall only follow the Way, for my name is Jealous. If you follow the Way, it will go well with you. But if you do not, you shall be stricken from this earth and be forgotten, like a field of grain consumed by the locusts. For the Way is life, but the path of the unclean is death.

*

I come from the House of God, in terms of the language we employ. Bethel is my home, and it has been the home of the workings of the Way for generations. In our tongue, *Beth* is the second letter, the first, *Aleph*, being reserved for the blameless, the Jealous one, the one unseen and with a voice that inks the pages of our people's past. What were my people.

In the songbook of the Way there is a passage that is dedicated to *Beth*, the origin of my home. *How can a man keep his way pure? By keeping it according to the words of the Way... I will mediate on thy precepts, and regard the Way. I shall delight in the statutes, and I shall never forget the words.*

Bethel is a sacred place, a place to be proud of coming from, of being from, or of passing through. This has always been true. But this is not true this day.

*

Now lift up your eyes and look from the place where you are, from Bethel, northward and southward and eastward and westward; for all the land you see, I will give it to you and your descendants forever. And I will make your descendants as the dust of the earth, so that if anyone can number the dust of the earth, then your descendents can also be numbered. Arise! Walk in the Way and all of this shall be yours.

*

It is simple to track the narrative of my home town. The story of my home, the walls and the people who once loved me within them, is more difficult for me to see. My mother seems to know the story, to have it committed to her aging mind, her faith-sodden heart. She is not at all clouded by love because she has long since watched that blown away for certainty. Her son is evil. Her son is of Gehenna. Damned because he has left the path, because he has forgotten the words, because he knows nothing of the Way.

That is her story, a story, but it is not the story. I know of the Way. I am the one who clears the road. I am the keeper of the Way, but how to explain to the woman who gave you life, the keeper of the womb where you unknowingly prepared for the first death, that it is your knowledge of the Way that has cast you away. How do you explain to your hate full mother that you love her, that you still love the idea of the Way, the idea the first one held to so dearly as he sat against that rock, alone and staring into the first void rendered by the Way, watching his people walk into the promise. That you long only for a deeper reckoning of this life. That you deserve to be loved because you are her son. That you deserve to be heard because you are alive.

*

This is the land which I swore to Abraham, Isaac, and Jacob, saying, "I will give it to your descendants." I have let you see the Way with your eyes, but you shall never go there with your body. This is the place where you shall die, but my people shall live forever.

*

Ever since the first Crossing, the Way has needed men like me, men who will handle the detritus of the Jealous one. But we are not told of in the words that my mother needs me to follow, or sung of in the songs that echo through the empty spaces of our meeting tents. We are the lost, the redacted, the erased, because we are the breathing reminders that the Way is narrow and sharp and lethal as any sword of war. The Way makes heroes of a few, and bodies of the many. Heroes can be sung about. Wine goblets are clashed and harps and lyres are plucked for the names we are told to know. But bodies must be cleansed and discarded so they can be forgotten, and that is dirty work to do, and while death may be inevitable, decency is not, whether living and feasting on the full table of youth or resting withered in my hands. It is my task to rescue the dignity that those who once lived can no longer claim for themselves. The Way. Today. No. I am not that man.

*

Today we heard of a new Crossing taking place on the outskirts of Bethel. We did not, no one could have known, what this Crossing would create. Not even I, a man who still believes that a knowledge of what has come before will make you unclean, and will make you see. Today I was blinded again because to truly see the world the Way has made is too close to hearing again that my mother is sickened by my life.

The reports came early in the morning. Young lads, messengers, came running to town to share the word.

"Elijah has been lifted up on high! The Way has blessed him and saved him from the taste of Sheol! He shall never rot, just as the Way has promised."

"How is this so?" a woman asked the boys. "All must find a home in the dust, do they not?"

"A great fiery horseman, in a chariot greater than any of the Pharaohs of before, fell down from the sky and snatched him up! Praise to the Jealous one who takes to him what he wishes."

"But what of us, then?" a crippled asked from his slump. "Who will keep us on the Way if Elijah has been taken?"

"Ah, patience old man," one of the lads said. "We have not arrived at the Crossing yet. But first give us drink and allow our breath to catch up with our words."

*

For I will not leave you until I have done what I have promised. And you shall call this place Bethel because this is the house of God and the gate to the Way. Now set here a stone so that this place will be known and remembered and my words shall not be forgotten and the Way to my house shall be marked. So that my people shall abide until the end of this earth.

*

Words can be stones. My mother gave me a letter this day. I must rewrite this letter, word for word, stone for stone, before I can rebuild this day the way it must be.

Son, former one. Today I have been reading. Reading. A thing to do. Things are done to do. Son. Son. Son. No, I mean that. Read this. My mind is very read. No. Pain, son. Much of it. There is no one here to do this for me. Isn't this your job, son?

And then the messengers, the lads, told us of the new prophet. Elisha is his name.

"His mantle, Elijah's mantle, it was given to Elisha in a double portion. He is now greater than the one before. The Way has a bright and morning star. We will be given a fiery leader of the Way!"

The youths could barely breathe.

*

Isn't this your job, son.

*

Do this for me, son.
Read this, son.
No one here, son.
Former son.

*

I do not know how to tell her that I am sorry. Now that she is gone.

*

There is a song my people have sung for centuries when a loved one has died. But I do not know if I can sing this song for my mother because I do not know if it applies.

But I will try at this precise moment. I will sing the song and see if, hear if, feel if it is a song to be sung for her.

There is no way to know weather. Know way to be the earth. Young man, young woman, there is no way to know while you are alive. You can only be alive while you are. Now lay the one you love down to die, as that is what must. Use your will, and use your heart, but do not use your mind for this will unmake you too soon.

Sing of the Way, sing of the Way, sing of the Way down the uphill road to Sheol, where we all must end. Sing this day.

*

My mother is not the one I love. It is you. This is a song for you. You must listen carefully, as carefully as I must sing to you.

*

I tend to the dead, as I have said. This is never easy work, but it is at least always necessary, somehow. But when it is Yahweh who is behind the murder of that many young, innocent, foolish boys, when you, when I, have to place my hands on that many bloody gashes in the bodies of that many youths, because of the awful pride of one man, and the ruthless power of one god, the blindness of the Way, the Way that forced my mother to kill her love for me, and then to kill herself, when this is the work the day asks of you, what is it you do. This.

The story is simple. You may already know it by now. Elisha, the new prophet and leader of the Way, Yahweh's chosen one, was walking down the road to Bethel. On his way he came across a group of young boys who, being the dumb runts they were, began to mock the prophet about his premature bald head. Elisha was upset, but instead of using the moment of youthful thoughtlessness to teach the lads a lesson, instead of giving them the gift of instruction or wisdom, he laid them waste. He, using the great power of Yahweh, invoking the name of the Way, called forth she bears from up the mountain to come down and rip the boys, these little human beings created in the very image of Yahweh, this all-too human god, to tear and shred the boys to pieces.

And that is where I come in. On the morning of my mother taking her life, I cleaned up the remnants of these children, and now I go to tell their mothers of their former sons.

The Way must be held accountable.

EYMAN'S PLIGHT

And Yahweh said to Job:
Shall a faultfinder contend with the Almighty?
Anyone who argues with God must respond.

Job 40: 1-2

Work worries me. My wife says I need to learn to separate my professional life from my private life, but that is a very difficult thing to do. My professional life is, from my point of view, my personal life. Or at least the two are inextricably connected. My wife, she says that a man must be able to live his life at home and leave work to rest until the next morning. She says that even the sun takes time off. But she is wrong because that is not true.

I understand my wife's concerns. I truly do. And I can see her point about letting go of work from time to time. I do love my family. I have two beautiful girls and a small piece of land, for which I am very grateful (for the record) that is enough to sustain a few oxen and some cattle. It is a good life I have at home and I am thankful for it. I love my wife and she is beautiful. Some might say striking. I would. It is not that I am obsessed with work, or even that I find my worth or my (let's say), identity, in my work. That is not it at all. It is more that work will not leave me. Work stays on me, like, well, like when you wake up in the night sweating and you cannot quite get the blanket off your legs and arms because your body has cleaved to the sheets. That is what work is like in my mind.

I do appreciate my job. Let me be very clear about that. Very much. I have had the honor of working in my position for the Divine Assembly now for many years. It is hard to say how many. It is one of the blessings and the curses (of course I say "curse" only for the sake of relative opposition) of my position in the Assembly – time can twist. Days and years and years and days, they can dance. It is quite wonderful, actually, to watch how the Assembly weaves things together. And, then again, unravels. There is a symmetry.

My wife cannot be privy to all of this – my work – which is why I have a difficult time explaining to her why my attention seems to drift often from our evening meal.

"Eyman!" she calls to me, me somewhere off in the East, though sitting in front of the food she has prepared. "Eyman! You are home now. It is time to focus on your family, remember?"

And I do remember. Honestly, I do. And I do want to hear about her day and our girls and what is going on with our neighbors. I do care about these things, the pieces of our life we are building together. But there are larger things at work. At my work, indeed, and things I cannot explain to her because I am not allowed.

That is why I have taken up this journal. It is time I make a concerted effort to separate my professional life from my private life, and to do that, several other items need to be separated as well. For one, when I think of work I often think in terms of "we" – what "we" did this or that meeting. But I do not *do* anything.

I have no power in the Assembly. So, it is what *they* do. But still, there remains a sense of belonging that I feel, and that troubles me. Now that I think of it, what is this I am doing now? Am I writing to me? Or to you? Well, these are questions. Aught I write to *her*? To my little girls? I am, at the moment, unsure. I am not writing for the Assembly. That is my professional life and this is about separation for the sake of understanding, for the sake of my private life. My private life needs some sorting, but recently I have seen and heard things that have only confused me further.

*

I feel that I should back up in case someone might read this at some point when things that I assume are known no longer assumed or known. That is something the Assembly rarely considers. Another beginning when their rules have changed. But I do consider this possible reality, but only in my mind. While I am at work I always assume what they assume as if they will be the powers of the earth until the end. As if they will always be. I have the advantage (let us say) of knowing of mortality, or at least of being mortal, and thus my mind naturally lends itself to ends. It is what makes – well, I will leave those thoughts – that is something altogether different from my professional life in the Assembly, and that is what I think I might spend some time with, for now.

My name is Eyman (as you might recall, my wife calls me Eyman [!]) and I am the clerk or scribe or executive assistant for the Divine Assembly – or more simply – the helpmate to the civic gathering of the Gods of the Heavens and Earth. That is interesting. I have never explained it before. My arms are cold and bumpy. That is quite interesting.

My job, in a very layman's sense, is to be present at all the meetings of the Assembly, to take down the minutes (so to speak, of course), and to keep record of the deliberations and decisions thereby made and to archive these records. I also get coffee, but they always ask this of me with respect. I am grateful for that.

It is disconcerting, but in all honesty (what else would a journal be good for, in that sense) I cannot properly remember how or why I was chosen for this position. Meaning, in part, that there does not seem to be any interview or application process in my memory. Of course, I have memories before my work began with the Assembly (not any that I can exactly *place* at the moment, but memories nonetheless) and, as you already know, I do have a life away from the Assembly (I did meet my wife away from work, et cetera), but I do not have any rigid notion of my beginning as Eyman, the clerk (Clerk, really). It will come to me in time.

The Assembly is really astonishingly revolutionary, if you think about it (although that is quite an awkward phrase, now that I read it over). For the longest time, it is said (there was no Eyman then to put it all down and file it away so neatly) people wandered about discovering their own questions and developing answers for the various plights they found themselves in (i.e. noticing a god), but there was no organization. No diplomacy. No regulatory processes, and those, as we all now well know, are the basic building blocks of civilization. The Gods saw the turmoil and unrest this was creating. Their needed to be some semblance of consolidation of power, or at least a venue (some say forum, I suppose) where the powers of creation could come together and make things better.

Certainly, as I'm sure you might imagine, there have been snags along the way.

(Now that I think hard on the matter, I am unsure. It seems we have always been, so to speak, at work. But clearly our records show there was chaos. Chaos, at first. Before us).

Equality is difficult to come by. We all know this from our own private lives (aha, see, it is already helping as I thought it would). In our daily interactions we strive to be equitable to our wives and children and friends. But this is not always easy, or possible, and this is true among the members of the Assembly as well. This should not shock you. The first and persistent problem is who gets to be in charge.

At the moment (if I may be so brazen to use such a word in this context) the leader of the assembly is Yahweh, the most active and ambitious god of the Hebrew people. He is really something. A wonder to watch at work. A constant puzzle, which, for a man like me, is fascinating. And let me add, for what it is worth, I say "puzzle" only in the most laudatory of senses. Yahweh has accomplished an impressive list of work since he planted Eden. That alone would have landed him a seat, but a power like Yahweh could not stop there. But, before I go too far in my speaking of our current leader, there are other honorable members who sit in the Assembly – the *sacra elohim* – as they prefer to be called. "Members" has sort of a pedestrian connotation, does it not?

Let me just see how well memory serves me and I will make a little list. I will start with the goddesses. All lovely in their own way. I do not tell my wife this as she tends to be jealous, but in reality (which is what is important anyhow) she has nothing to worry about. One touch from one of the *elohim* and I am nothing but dirt and ash. I understand this. And in my work one must become adept at walking (at times, crawling, in a sense) amongst the jealous.

There is Shaushka of Ninevah who focuses most of her work on the land. There is Bendis of Thracia who, if I can be frank, focuses on her face. But who could blame her? And of course, there is Isis of Egypt – the Pharaoh Duster, who lays to waste all that she allures. Quite powerful and convincing. Quite persuasive.

Among some of the other major actors in the Assembly are Ashtoreth of Sidonia, Milcom – god of the Ammorites (he and Yahweh have some epic spats), Chemosh of Moab, An of Sumeria, and lest I forget, there is the insatiable Enki, the Drunken god of the Crescent. Enki loosens the silt – always a character. He is not really the true God of his people. That honor belongs to Enlil, but he is often too busy and allows Enki to sit for him, when he is able. Often even when he is not, and that can be humorous, but only in the most respectful of ways. The cast of the Assembly does have some flux. Some come and go. Like in any other professional sphere, some are more prompt and professional than others. But I can assure you, I am always on time. First to come and last to leave.

Lastly, but not least (on several levels), is Marduk. I do not want to speak in a dishonorable way, or to be offensive in case younger eyes find these words, but Marduk is an impressive deity. The Snake, some say. He is always respected.

But that is enough of the technicalities. Lists are tedious. But you must remember, this is a list no other man has. If people knew their gods met like this there would be renewed chaos, something all of these great powers have wrestled to the ground at one point or another in their careers. You must understand now, or at least must be able to feel the shade of the thing, why it is hard for me to forget about my work.

*

I must be careful. I am realizing as I go back and forth through this – careful of not calling work a job. I find myself confused enough lately and I do not want to add to my own confusion, especially here, where words are supposed to help me. One must have allies. One must at least have oneself.

So, we do good work, and have for some time. Chances are if you are reading this, if there are still a collection of you out there at some time when these pages become known, chances are you have heard of the Assembly and the work we do.

The Tree was a traumatic time. Everything was in an uproar – absolute chaos, even, some tried to argue, worse than before the Planting. Some blamed Yahweh for the Tree, and that, I must say very clearly, is simply not fair. He saved us from the scandal the wild ones caused with their seeds. I must be wary now, for there are some names not to be spoken (and although these words are still silent, I must be careful, vigilant). But when the *adamah* (that, I think, is a safe name) ate of the Tree – the Tree, for the record, that the Majority of the Assembly was against in the first place – and gained the knowledge of East and West something had to be done. I can recall the meetings more clearly than the birth of my wonderful girls.

"We must kill them now!" Marduk boiled.

"Let us simply see what happens," purred Enki.

Yahweh was silent.

"Perhaps," said Isis, "this will be useful."

But Yahweh knew. Knew the *adamah* must not have both life and mind, breath and soul. Knew it as if he saw what it would require of him, of us. Then he spoke.

"See, the *adamah* has become like one of us, knowing good and evil, and now, he might reach out his hand and take also from the tree of life, and eat, and live forever. These things must be guarded. That, now, is our task."

He was the most forward thinking of all the *elohim*. And so the *adamah* were banished and the sentries were set, and Yahweh proved his administrative might. My hand seemed to float on its own accord as I took down the proceedings, as if I did not even have to look down, instead able to look about the Assembly and see the codification of the beginning of a new day breaking forth on the faces circled about me.

The dawning, as I once overheard (in no way eavesdropping) Isis call, of the unknowable race. She was right, I must admit, on some counts. Understanding became flexible.

New chaos ran down our desire for order and peace. The *ad-amah's* decedents were strong and stubborn, hard working with their bodies and lost in their thoughts, often without reflection as to what their creators might be thinking, as if they really had no ideas on the matter. They lived fast yet long lives, days full of the ranting of bodies joined and tore apart, days of hunt and toil and fire, and nights of forcible death and the cries of birth. Brutal times. Times that still, to this day, make my skin quiver to recall. But we took care of this, too. We washed away the filth that had been gathering around the far flung edges of the Garden.

Babel was also a sight to behold. As if they, now that they had seen what the Assembly could do to them if they were to continue to live in their confusion, were now desperate to find a way into our rooms. As it is with them (it seems to me from my observations over time) they wanted too much. They wanted to know God. They wanted to be remembered.

"Let them build," Enlil said at the time. "Let us see what it is they can do."

"Listen to them speak," Shaushka said. "They have one tongue. One collection of words. They are learning. They are growing up. Isn't this what we wanted of them? To use the earth? To see what they could make of things?"

Yahweh's silence was easily broken.

"Look, they are one people, and they have one language," Yahweh boomed as if he cared nothing for the previous words because they were not his own (and understandably so). "This is only the beginning of what they will do; nothing that they propose to do will be impossible for them. Come, let us go down, and confuse their language there, so that they will not understand one another's speech."

And it was so. Like frogs hopping on coals. The Great Scatter.

This is our work. And, until recently, I have been proud of it. It has seemed good.

*

I thought I would write more this morning, but I hear my girls gurgling awake and that seems to be the place to put my effort, for now.

*

Among the *sacra elohim* he is called the Adversary – *hasatan*. He has been called many things and served many purposes. Held other positions, too. He is unlike any other in the Assembly.

He has always been quite kind to me. Always calls me Eyman. Never "Clerk." We do not have long conversations, certainly, and I would not be so brash as to say that I "know" him very well, but I have often got the impression that he, well, I suppose I feel like in some way he recognizes the importance of my position.

He has a free mind. That is the best way I can think to describe him. He represents the *adamah's* descendants. He seems to recognize their importance, too. Or, more to the point, their existence. Not that they do exist, of course. The Assembly knows that well enough. I mean something else.

He is not always present at meetings. In fact, his presence is quite elusory in an administrative sense. He will be at meetings then not. His attention is rarely kept. And although this is quite frustrating for a man of my sentiments, it is also interesting. He often roams the earth.

But, it is critical that I make this clear, he is called the Adversary for very appropriate reasons. Yahweh has other, stronger names. But again, to be fair, the two of them have deeper ties than most. He is a disruptor of the peace. Quite adversarial to much of our programs and courses of action. Because he is not as wary of chaos as we are. He thinks of the future differently.

I have always had great respect for him, though, in a professional sense. I am speaking here only in a professional sense, of course, and keeping my private concerns separate (as any healthy man must do). I see his role in the Assembly as necessary. New perspectives. I think all policies are bettered by fresh insight and perspective. Assessments. Outcomes. Rubrics. All these very important categories for experience and legislation require a variance in perspectives. It is a deeply held professional belief I hold. And he has been, quite often, the voice of their race. A volunteer on their behalf. A defense (at least if you were to ask him).

So, outside of the context of the Assembly he might not properly be called the Adversary. That really, is all I am trying to say.

I see this will have to be a draft.

*

I think I must write what happened. I have been waiting to understand it before I tell of it. But perhaps, in this case, the processes that I trust must be reversed.

The Adversary was late. Most, or at least those we were expecting, were all on time. Present and accounted for. Cups were full and steamy, my notepad was crisp. Pen full on ink. Time to get to work.

Yahweh said a few things. Things were calm about the earth. The smell of sacrifice was heavy and assuring in the halls. Prayers were being lifted from every corner. Then in he walks.

"Where have you come from?" Yahweh asked of him, perturbed (as he should have been).

The Adversary looked at him, almost scoffing with his slow moving lips (as if to say you know that I know that you all know very well where I have been – at least, that was just my impression), then spoke. "From going to and fro on the earth, and from walking up and down on it."

Then Yahweh said, "Have you considered my servant Job? There is no one like him on the face of the earth, a blameless and upright man who fears his God and turns away from evil."

The Adversary seemed surprised, as if, perhaps, Yahweh was putting forth some kind of challenge.

"Yes, I know Job. But does he fear his God for no reason? Have you not put a fence around his existence? Given him nothing but the peaceful and prosperous side of life? You have taken the rest away. He has no reason to doubt. Is this truly, even, a life you speak of? You take such pride in this? Do you have the courage to test it?"

"Do not question my Courage in my Rooms!" Yahweh quaked as he burst from the chair. "Do what you will to this Job you speak of! Do what you will, fiend! But do not take his life!"

The Adversary's face was calm. "Yes, yes. Of course not his life. There would be no point in that, now would there."

*

But Yahweh could not wait for the Adversary. His patience was spent. Job lost everything but his life, surely, but no one mentions this part of it at work. I will only say it here. Here this thought will be safe. But it is not even a thought, or a wrong, to say it. It is simply an observation of fact. I cannot be held responsible for that. I cannot. It is this. Job lost everything, or, rather, had it taken from him, but it was not by the Adversary. Here, I will simply transcribe the transcripts. That will be safe.

Here, here it is. THE FIRE OF GOD FELL FROM HEAVEN AND BURNED UP THE SHEEP AND THE SERVANTS AND CONSUMED THEM. And here, here is another section from the records. AND SUDDENLY A GREAT WIND CAME ACROSS THE DESERT, STRUCK THE FOUR CORNERS OF THE HOUSE, AND IT FELL ON THE YOUNG PEOPLE,

AND THEY ARE DEAD. You see? It was not the Adversary. His power, if you can even call it that, is not that of fire and wind and water. His power is not elemental in that way. He simply has words. He is a speaker of ideas. So, it was Yahweh. Yahweh did this to Job. And, if I can once again simply point out a fact of the proceeding (and certainly not go so far as to draw any implications other than this very simple observation), that Yahweh is the one who brought up Job in the first place. I did not understand this. And I have no one to ask about it. But there was also a second meeting.

This day was eerily like the first. The Adversary came in late and Yahweh questioned him. In fact, the conversation was so much like the first, so actually identical, it was almost as if Yahweh had forgotten all about it. This, of course, I think I can say with some certainty, is not the case. He did not forget it. Simply an oddity of the way words work. Things are often repeated.

But there was a difference. After the Adversary told Yahweh where he had been Yahweh brought up Job again.

"Have you considered my servant Job? There is no one like him on the earth, a blameless and upright man who fears his God and turns away from evil." Then it was as if this sparked his memory, for new words were spoken.

"He still persists in his integrity, although you incited me against him, to destroy him for no reason!"

But this is not what happened, as I am sure you recall. It simply is not the truth.

The Adversary ignored this. He let Yahweh put the terms as he wished to put them. Then he responded, "Skin for skin. All that people have they will give to save their lives."

"Very well," Yahweh said, appeased at these words. Proud, it seemed. "His flesh is in your power. But save his life."

Then the Adversary looked at me, (I swear this) and winked. "That, my old friend, is what this is all about."

*

My life began when my first daughter was born. That is how it feels to me. I had many other experiences before this. I had worked for the Assembly for what I assume was a long time before Emie was born. Perhaps eons. I never cared to count. But when you have a child years begin to matter. Half years. Quarter years. Days have significance. She is now six years and seven months. In five short months she will be seven.

My younger daughter we call Rook. Her real name is Rubey, but Emie could never pronounce it correctly. The long soft intended ending of her sister's name was always given that curt, shortened finish. And it stuck. So, she is Rook. Emie and Rook.

It is a wondrous thing to be a father. More work than I thought was possible, but then again, when you do not have children, and are really only responsible for your own life, you often feel overwhelmed. One life is a demanding thing. Then you have a wife and that becomes in some ways one new life to manage, but in truth, it is like three new lives to manage. You have your own self (you think), and your wife to think of, then you have you and your wife's life to nurture. Then you have a child and then children and the numbers of lives you then must lead and live become unwieldy. And worth it. Fatherhood has given my life days, again. And a depth.

They grow up before your eyes like phantoms, and even though their existence gives you back a sense of time, the speed of their changes makes a fool of your sentimentality. Once you learn to love them they have gone off and become someone completely else.

I actually love that, too.

This is why my wife is so concerned, and I do understand that. I do. She also recognizes how fast they are growing – how new the world seems to them each day – how important it is to their development to have an attentive father and mother that they can depend upon to guide them through the pitfalls of growing up. She often says that we need to make every transition *together.* She says I spend too much time worrying about work, about providing, about *my* life, and that I need to spend more of that energy on *their* lives – which should all be *our lives!* It is impossible to keep track of. I am a man of splinters.

I am a good man. A good father. A good employee. And that is the problem. I do not know how to speak of the problem. I do not think I have words for these things.

If I speak of my worries to directly, you see, I will no longer be a father. Better to be a father in pieces, I think. Do you think.

*

Gird up your loins like a man and I will question you. Will you ever put ME in the wrong? Will you condemn ME that you might be made right? Have you an arm like ME? Can your voice thunder like MY voice thunders to you now?

Look at Behemoth. Do you see it? It has strength in its loins. Do you? It can make its tail stiff as cedar. Can you? Look how tight the sinews of its flesh are stitched together. Its bones are tubes of bronze. Its limbs are bars of iron. You are simply molded flesh. A container.

Can you draw out Leviathan with a hook, or press down his tongue with your rope? Can you rope this beast with your noose, or pierce its jaw with your blade? Will the monster cry out to you for mercy? Will its words be spoken softly to you, oh man? Will this Creature make promises to you? Do you think the wild things of the world will serve you – oh man who was made and had no power in his making? Will you play with it on a leash and give it to your girls to play? Do you have that power?

On earth I am unequaled. I am King of the Proud.

What could Job say back to Yahweh now? What on earth could he respond.

I know YOU can do all things, and that no purpose of YOURS can be thwarted. I have uttered what I did not understand, things too much for me to hold or know. I had heard of YOU, but now I have seen YOU and the work of YOUR hands. I despise this life. I am only dust.

The Adversary, when questioned by Yahweh about what Yahweh hailed as a victory for Himself and the Assembly, had little to say. In fact, he said only this.

"Old brother. You have forgotten life. You have no ear for irony."

*

I do not want what I love to be taken
How can I hope to avoid
This is out of my hands
A man's toil should matter
I must work my way through this
I love my girls. I want them to live long happy lives.
I need to believe I can make this so
Chaos is still alive
I want to wash out my eyes
I am a man of unclean memories
What is this world we are making?

ROLL A GREAT STONE
TO ME TODAY

Do I lack madmen, that you have brought this one to
act the madman in my presence?

I Samuel 21:15

Some stories are more important than others. What makes them important, how we go about deeming importance, or who gets to do the deeming, all this can get to be, well, let us call it fluid. I know the story I want to tell you like it was the back of my hand, but even the back of my hand will not stay still. It grows, and it will shrink. The hair comes out like golden wheat, and soon it will dry and fall like the unneeded fibers of lost corn. Its color from year to year is re-invented by the elements, things I am told exist but do not see and rarely feel. And as the appearance of my hand will surely change, so will what lies below in the matter of its usefulness. Yet, I know this hand, and I know this story, but the more one knows a story, I now think, the more one is aware that one story can never exist. There has never been one story of any story. And I will never be in control of my hands, even if I memorize the names of hidden bones.

There are three main characters, or men, in this story, although many other extras were needed to give the thing the grand scope required for the importance to be grasped. Human beings need grandeur to feel worthy enough to keep breathing, a short reading of history seems to suggest. My first thought was to pretend to be one or more of the three men so that they could try to tell their own story, from their own angle of importance, but now I, as I sit down to tell something, I cannot see any use for pretending. It strikes me as being the first real trouble with the other tellings of this story – this belief, or posture of the writer or the teller telling as if they *knew* any of this. As if they were actually in full control of the narrative. As if telling a story were like smoothing out concrete. As if reality has anything to do with *there*.

What you need to keep in mind as we go around this story together is that the origins of the story are ancient. Scholars argue about how ancient and attempt to use what they think of as textual science to prove just how ancient we are talking when we talk this story and stories like it. I am not a man of science, or knowledge, and I have ceased to be a man of argument, but what I do think will prove helpful if we are to enjoy the story at all is to assume that the first tellings of it were so far back in human history that most of our ontological conceptions are far different, not to say better or improved, but certainly changed, since the King decided it was time to name a king. That is the other trouble, I think, where we lose track of the purpose of story – when we try to use stories to prove anything, especially things like the family line of a savior of the world.

If we can agree that stories are not historical arti-facts to be dusted and dissected, that stories and ideas do not flow through the pipeline of time that we reconstruct to suite our unique notions of progress every generation, if we can agree that stories exist only insofar as there is a teller and a listener, and that each subject remakes the story and gnaws upon any wished for objective core, often without truly *knowing* that is what is being presently *done*, than the beginning is not that important, as it were. It is just a matter of convention and necessity. Otherwise, how could we ever *get going* in the first place? What could the first place really be? Where would it end, and the second place begin? With that in mind, I would like to tell you this.

*

During some time that is now ours but then was not, there was the King. The King began with no kingdom at all, and that is no way for a King to live, so the King began construction of a kingdom. This took quite some time and there were many logistical snags along the way, but the King, for all his faults, was very very persistent and ambitious. This kingdom was going to happen, like it or not. But the King, never having a kingdom or any subjects before now, had no idea what to expect when things got put into motion. He was playing it be ear, yet he had these stern expectations about how things were supposed to go, and he often got extremely angry when they did not go the way he wanted. Trouble was, he created subjects without knowing that what he truly wanted was objects. Trouble is there is a difference.

Sadly, there was no one to teach the King, as he was one of a kind and without equal in power or stature. The King lost his kingdom and his subjects several times along the way, but his ultimate magnetism always led him back to them, or they to him. But even though the King had a kingdom and many subjects and all the control in the world, he was still not satisfied. Something was missing. He was lonely and confused, and guilty for being either. He tried to connect with the great men of his kingdom, the exceptional sorts who towered above the rest, whether in intellect or valor or size or sheer brute force, but they always let him down in some way. They did not listen exactly to what he said, or they proved to be fragile, or they proved to be mortal. The King, being eternal, could not grasp the temporal world he made for himself.

After many years of living under a clearly unhappy King, the people got wise to the fact that they had their own minds, in large part thanks to the situations the King made possible way back when, and because they were given the great gift of their own minds, however indirectly, from the King, they decided it was high time they used them and made some demands of their own. So, the people went to the man of the hour that was the King's special guy and said, "old special man of the hour, we no longer want to live under the King. We want our own king, a man like us, a guy who understands our us-ness, what it feels like to be made, what it hurts like to be dying, what it tastes like to be alive." So, the old man of the hour went to the King and relayed the wishes of the people. The King, in classic King fashion, went berserk. Then, after all that was out and the old man of the hour heard the King rave, the King got a bit petulant as he was also prone to do, and pouting, in a none too endearing tone not fit for the King of the world, said, "Fine, old man of the hour. We shall give them a king of their own." And this, as you can imagine by now, set off this whole chain of events that, in terms of a wider scope of what we like to think of as History, was like a mammoth cliff falling into the only ocean ever known to man, starting this newborn wave that would crash into another land of storytelling man way down the line, and the King would still be standing, although aged some, and altogether different in terms of values and emotiveness and whatnot. But for now, we will try to focus on the King and king and the other king, and at some point, if we have the energy, we can get to the end where the wave breaks and the King of kings and all the rest. When the King became the Father.

The King, at least part of him, was glad to be rid of the day to day aspects of ruling his people. Maybe, he thought, it will be good for them to have a king they can relate to. So, the King sent off the old man of the hour to a no man's house, a man of little importance, who happened to have a very impressive son. This son was the most handsome man in the kingdom at this time, and some said the most handsome man of any time, although come on now, who could really know such a thing as that. He was also very large – so large that he was taller than any other man in the kingdom only measuring from his shoulders up, which is to say, his neck and his head were taller than any grown man, and you can imagine the remainder. He was not a bright fellow, even with all of that headspace, but he was diligent and sincere in his daily chores, dependable, and if not chaste, one could at least say he was vigorous.

But like all men chosen to be kings of this world, it was his energy that made him chosen, and his energy that made him exile.

It is important to note presently, before we go on, that before this king, the old man of the hour was as close to a king as the people had ever known. He was not a great man of might, or a military mind, but he was a man of vast and dark knowledge, a man that was left alone as a child to learn in the holy house of the King, a man who was abandoned by his father, and taught by the high holy one of the King at that time, which is to say, the old man of the hour, when he was young, was raised by the old man of the hour then. This tends to be the way these things go, power being such a contagion.

But now, right before the King told the old man of the hour to pick the first king, the King tried to set up the old man of the hour's sons with leadership roles amongst the people, a sort of decision council to be set up instead of a King – a non-royal parliamentary dynasty, as some might see it. The people, however, were having none of that. These two sons, they were throwing their proverbial weight around in a town called Beersheba[1] and the people did not appreciate this. It showed them that the old man of the hour's time had come and gone, that he was too much an old man, and not enough of the hour, and that he could not control his sons, and his sons could not be kings.

"Give us a true king!" they demanded. One must ask what they knew as a true king, never having the pleasure of having one.

"You have the King, and you say you want a king? You are a confused and obstinate people," the old man of the hour told them.

"Make us like all other kingdoms of the world, for they have kings to lead them, and our king may judge us, and fight our battles."

It was clear what the people wanted, so the King sent his old man of the hour, what the people thought of as a seer, to the town of Zuph, to meet with the man that would be king.

The King was not one to do things simply – he was not interested in sending his man to choose the first king in any straightforward way. Instead, and this was often the way with the King, he set up a series of events, a human set of strings and pulleys, in order to show how in charge he was.

The man to be the first king was out looking for some donkeys that his father had lost. He traveled from town to town, but could not find the donkeys, even with his watchtower frame. Finally, he got to Zuph, where he saw a woman drawing at a well.[2]

---

1   The name of this town might be of some interest at some point near the end
2   The fact that he was on a donkey mission and has a conversation with a woman drawing water at a well might also be of some interest down the road.

"I have seen no donkeys," she said, "but there is a great seer of the King in our town, and he may know where your donkeys are."

With this, the man to be king went out to find the seer, and the seer knowing the man was coming, went out to see the man, all the while having the King in his ear, communicating with him from afar.

There are many tales of how the King was able to do this, but I am not a man to tell you which is which. The way I see it, if the King in the story could make the kingdom, than he also has some license with the laws of the kingdom – he never actually being truly *in* the kingdom – which is why, I suppose, the people, in their wisdom unawares, would want to have a king with them *in* the living of their lives.

When the soon to be king saw the seer, he said, "Tell me where the seer is, so that I may ask him about the donkeys."

And the seer said, "I am the seer of the King. Do not worry about the donkeys, for they have been found. Listen closely to me, for the next day of your life is full." Then the seer took out a flask of oil and poured it over the almost king's head and said, "The King has put you in charge of all the kingdom, and you shall be the first king, and you shall rule with the blessing of the King."

"But I am from the smallest tribe, and from a no man's family, and I have done no great deeds, and so how is it that you speak to me as if I am a great man?"

One might say – well, look at that head of yours, for starters! But seers do not say things like that.

"This is what the King has decided. You will go to the tomb of the first crying mother, and there you shall find men who will tell you that your donkeys are safe. Then, you will go past the

Oak Tree at Bethel, and there you will come across three men[3] and they will have three small calves and three loaves of bread, and also some wine, and you will accept all that they give you. Then, you will go up to the Hill where the enemy is encamped, but before you get to the camp of the foul ones, a group of prophets of the King will come down the Hill with tambourines and harps and lyres, singing songs of deliverance, and it is then, and only then, that the Breath of the King will come upon you, and you will be a changed man, a new man, no longer the man of the no man's home, but now the man who will be the king of the King's people."

The man was silent. And all those things did happen.

At the end of the man's journey he was allowed to go home to find his family and the donkeys, safe and sound. Soon after, the seer came and gathered them all, and brought them for the Day of Annointing, where the people would finally be introduced to their new and very first king. All the people were gathered, and the seer was dressed in his absolute nicest special man of the hour robes, and the man's family was in the crowd, confused and proud, and the seer said in his loudest and most official of memorable day voices, "You have asked the King for a king of your own, and the King has heard your cry, and the King has answered. You rejected the King as your king, but he is merciful, and today shall give you the king of your hearts. Now, separate yourselves by your tribes and your clans, and present yourself before your King in the order in which you were called, and meet the man who will be your king from this day forward!"

At this, the crowd divided, seamless as the marching of a caterpillar, and in only a few moments to the naked eye, the crowd

---

3   The number three becomes almost annoyingly significant throughout this story and those that it spawned, and the fact that the just about king has to go to Bethel is also really something – Bethel is like one of the King's favorite places to do really dramatic Kingly things.

was re-ordered according to the twelve early fathers of the earliest sons.

"Now, bow to the man who will be king!"

The crowd bowed, exhilarated, ready more than a drowning man's lungs for air to meet the man who would be their king.

No one came.

The seer looked around, and the man was not coming. They waited.

Finally, the King in the seer's ear said, in a near snicker, "check the baggage."

And there was the man so close to being king, hiding in the refuse. The seer grabbed him, and dusted him off, and presented him to the people.

"Do you see him! This is the man the King has chosen for you! Surely there is no one like him amongst all of the people!"

And the people roared in unison unknown since the days before the great storm, "Long live the king!"

*

That is the first part of the story, but now that I have set it aside for some time and come back to it again, I feel that my story, or my interest in telling the rest of the story, is over, or spent, or hiding in the refuse, cowardly, too. If I could only know if you still wanted to hear more, or how you might want the rest conveyed to you, then I trust I would have the courage to continue. But I do not even know if there is a you, and you certainly cannot be convinced of me, in any useful sense, at least up until now, with what you have been offered, or denied, it may seem.

A synopsis.

The king had a rough go of things, mostly because the King found a candidate that he found more suitable for the position. The more one follows the stories of the King and the second king, one might decide that suitor is the most appropriate term. As the story goes the first king was not cut out for the position, mostly because the King forced him into madness, in order to smooth the way for the second king, because the second king was truly exceptional in the King's sight, although he is described in an eerily similar fashion to his predecessor, "young, handsome, and from a place one would not expect to find a king in the making." His claim to fame was throwing a stone into the head of a giant, the stone that cleared the way for the victory of his people. An ancestor of this second king would also clear the way with a stone, but who his people were, are, or might be, this story has never been fully told. It is very much up in the air.

But back for a moment to the first king, who I seem to have a fondness for, more than I knew when I began to tell his story. And this is why. He was a man who was lifted up by the King only to be thrown down. He has for centuries been made a villain, and he seems to have known this would be so, because once he recognized he was done for, he said to his people, "roll to me a great stone today." As if he saw his open tomb all too clearly.

I, for a long time, have hated the King, mostly because of his caprice, the way he cruelly thrashes about his kingdoms and his kings, his subjects, his worlds, but now, as I sit back and wonder why I have spent so much of my mind on the stories that deal with the King, I must now ask why I hate the King so, when he had nothing to do with his part in the stories. The King did not write them, and the King did not tell them, and the King did not print them, and the King did not sell them. The King has been used as much as he used any one character in any of the stories I think of as *his*. But as we found out once we killed him off, the King never owned a thing.

So, as the story goes, the King was much more understanding of his second king. The King learned so much, one might say, that he disappeared for hundreds of years, only to come back as the Father – a much more subtle ruler, some would say.

And now I see that the blame is not the King's to carry, that forcing that burden on the King all these years, all these stories, is only doing to the King the very thing I have hated him for doing to many others, and to me. Because stories came out of the first consciousness as a revolt against blame, and use, and power, and control, and villainous certainty – the first stories were representations of will, a will to declare nothing and absolutely so other than that I am here, we are here, for now, at least. The King is as confused as the rest of us, just bigger, strong enough to hold the fears and hopes and hatreds of so many storyless human beings. And whose fault is that, in the end.

We long to know, and there has never been a shortage of those who are willing to tell us what to know, how to know, where to look, and then to call all that *belief*. Kings have always been good tools for building blinding towers, masked fathers, and the concealed sickles of certain fools, but now, I have to ask, if my hatred for the King is not the same sort of certainty. It may not be the King I hate, or even the stories of him that make me hate, and perhaps it is not the childish tellers of these stories, those who use the King to be kings themselves. Blame may not be the point of stories at all, someday. Someday the worship of heroes and hatred of villains may not be why stories rise or fall, last or disappear. Someday, but that is all still in the telling.

A REED SHAKEN

What did you go out into the wilderness to see?

Matthew 11:7

My Parents were fond of telling me different stories of my birth. They would never speak of such things while we were all three together, but often when one of them would have me to themselves, I would hear about my origins.

Father was always a quiet man, especially in the presence of mother. She was not an imposing figure in her speech, but rather a warrior of the eye. He was not a worthless man, not a man to have his mind led about by a woman. He was a priest in the line of Abijah, well respected in our town and further off, a man who stood in the holy places alone and survived. And that is where her story began.

Mother said that Father was doing his normal duties in the temple one day, walking among the praying people outside, listening to their cares before passing into the altar room to offer up incense to our God on their behalf. It was then that an angel of the Lord came to him, proclaiming that his wife would bear him a son, and that the son would be named John. Mother's face always gleamed as she recounted the angel's words, words she claimed her husband had told her much later on, once he was given back his speech.

The angel told him that this boy John, this John who writes this now, would be a great prophet to Israel, a new Elijah, a sober and righteous man of focus and refreshing for the people of the Lord. She would hold my hand with great strength and recount how this boy, how I, would be the messenger for the Messiah. How I, with the words of the Most High, would cut a path in our exile for the man to come to save us from the oppression that had stretched out before us as dry and far as a desert wind traveling the earth. I was to be the Messiah's trumpet. I was to give the people the ears they would need and the courage for the battle he would bring.

Mother's story was also like a great wind as it blew in and out of my memory, each telling having new gusts and lulls. Sometimes she would begin with Mary's visit after my father was told of my birth from the great Gabriel himself. "You see", she would say, "Gabriel also visited my friend Mary. You know Mary, do you not, my precious one? He came and told her of a son she would bear as well so that each of us, in the same year, would bear miracles. And these miracles, my dear boy, are you and your friend Jesus, and you will change our people into a people of promise once again. You will, together my son, together you and Jesus will give us back our place with the Lord."

Father never cried, as mother often did, when he told me his story. Father was not a man of great emotion. He would often tell me in whispers, "Your mother comes from the line of Aaron and thus she is fond of her own voice. This is the way of her people. I am fond of the spirit, son, and the spirit will abide once the tongue has been cut out."

He would take me out to the Jordan from time to time and tell me of the traditions of our people. Sometimes we would fish and sometimes we would gather up rocks to see who could find the stone without blemish. As a man now I can listen back to his sparse words and hear the song of a skeptic when he would talk of some of the prophets. I believe he was a sympathizer with King Saul, something he would never say in the Temple out of fear of reproach, but a sentiment he would hint at as we compared our stones.

"The Lord is not simple to hear and more difficult to understand, boy. Any man who seems to hear nothing but the Lord is a man you must watch with all the corners of your eyes. King Saul did not know this wisdom, and he was struck mad. Do not be as innocent or as ignorant, my son."

But before I could ever ask anything, or speak in any way to him, he would grab my finest rock and toss it into the water, right along the top, as if for a moment the rock was running on the surface.

Father would not say much about the time of his silence while I grew inside of mother. But he would often chuckle about the three months Mary stayed in our house after Gabriel made himself and the will of the Lord known to our two families. Father said he and Joseph became close friends during this time and that, though he was not a man of regret, he grieved deeply when Joseph chose to leave.

"A man can do nothing else than what he knows the Lord requires," he told me once. "Joseph was a good man. A man with the sensitivity of a priest. He knew he had to go and he knew why. I never doubted him."

Sometimes my father would speak not to me, but to his own heart.

"He was a good man. He knew what the boy meant to his marriage. He had courage few men will have."

Mother and Mary would bring the two of us together often. They would sit in our home and I could hear the fountain of laughter that came from their mouths. As I got older this happiness startled me. We were poor families. We lived amongst a poor people, under a wealthy and cruel tyrant. What did they have to hope in? What was this joy spring they had found? At times I would try to talk to Jesus about these things, but he was more interested in his own roads. He was not a boy who looked back to where we had come from. He was a new thing.

Our childhood together was a pleasant one in many ways. We would run in the streets and roust old dogs as they slept their last sleeps. We would talk to the merchants in the market and distract them so that some of the beggars might be able to grab a handful of figs or olives. We were simple boys without many acquaintances but with much energy and a sense of childish time that let us run without need. But everything was changed when he came back from the festival in Jerusalem.

We were twelve years old when the time came to go once again to the great city and celebrate Passover. This year would not be like the other years. Jesus stayed behind the caravan and worried everyone, especially Mary.

"The boy is gone. The boy, my boy is not here!" she cried.

Jesus was found in the Temple speaking with the teachers of the day. They say he spoke with a voice of a large wave that crashed on the wise men and loosened them from their seats. He spoke out of the throat of a man, out of an echoing deepness a child must not have.

I had heard this voice before, but only twice. Once, we were in the fields throwing rocks into a tree. Jesus threw one rock that fell back down alongside the body of a sparrow. We ran over to the bird and Jesus picked it up in his hands and squeezed as if he were going to crush the poor dead thing. Instead, he spoke into his palms and said, with the ocean's voice, "Little bird, now is not your time. My Father commands it. Rise up and fly again." And it obeyed. It obeyed his awful voice. The other time, even now as a man in prison I do not like to recount, but when time is like a short wick all must be made known. We were very young boys. The day was fading out and it was almost time to go in. Atop a roof of a neighbor boy's house we were drawing lots without a purpose. The neighbor boy called Jesus false at the game and in a blink of my eye the boy was off of the roof and trembling on the ground below. We rushed down and Jesus put one hand on the boy's head and another on his belly and said with the voice of a father into the pure white that covered the boy's eyes, "You are to rise now and guide your mouth." The boy ran off into his home and I into mine.

I never told anyone of this voice, but when he came back from the Temple he seemed to use it more often. "John, why would they not know that I would be in my Father's house? Where else would it be right for me to do my Father's business?" I did not answer. He did not ask the questions to be answered ever again.

As we came closer to the time of men we drifted apart. I spent more time with my father because I wanted to learn the tradition from his lips. In the beginning of this education I would invite Jesus to join us but he would simply say, with the voice of a young man, "Zechariah is your father and it is right you learn from him. I have my own Father who teaches me all from above." His eyes worried me but he had wisdom none of the other boys had, wisdom I did not have or even my father the priest. But father taught me well. He told me of the prophets and of the backsliding of Israel. He told me of the wrath of the Lord due to the sin of the people and that the Lord was not one to turn one's back upon. Jeremiah, Elijah, Isaiah, Nehemiah. These names he sowed into me and I felt nurtured by the stories he would let me hear.

"We are waiting, son," he would say, "for a great warrior who will come from the line of David. A warrior who will slay a giant much greater than any Goliath. This Warrior King, this Messiah, will come and rescue us from our captivity. He will come with a sickle to weed out the wheat from the chaff, and with a sword to cut the throats of all those who oppose the Lord our God. He will be the Lion of Judah, the hope of the Nation."

"When will we know, father?"

"We will know when we have heard the message from the wilderness. That is what the prophet Isaiah has told us through the mouth of the Lord. We have suffered for our sins. The day of our redemption is near, my son. Herod is not God. Herod will no longer be our God."

My father died with these beliefs, and once he was gone, I devoted myself to my own study, no longer having him as a guide. The Tanakh became my priest and I served it faithfully. I would try to tell my mother what I was learning, what I was coming to believe about my place in our tradition.

"Mother, our people need a leader. We do not belong in the world if we are citizens of Rome."

"John, you must let your father's ideas leave you now that he is gone. We are not a people to fight. We must trust in the Lord. He will save us."

"The Lord awaits our action. All his prophets have told us this much. We must read what the Lord has already done, what he has said through the mouths of the men of God!"

"We must wait, John, for Jesus. We must await the words of Gabriel to come to pass. And you must be patient, dear one, for you are a part of these words."

I left my mother with almost nothing for the wilderness. I brought the few scrolls I could carry in my sack, a skin of water, and a knife. I knew not for what I went; only that our people had once found freedom in the desert and that our prophets proclaimed a new beginning once more from this place. And the memory of my father. There I stayed, reading and surviving. I was fortunate to find the abandoned carcass of a camel at the beginning. The meat had gone rotten but the skin was good for clothes and warmth in the night. I had the Jordan to keep me cool and clean, and the locusts and bees sustained me. The Lord was building me.

The heat of the summer months became a constant enemy to my mind. I would cry out to the Lord to teach me or to kill me, to tell me of what I must repent to be of use to him. Silence was the friend of the heat and they both beat me with the blows of hosts. Eventually, travelers came across my camp, stricken by the bones of my ribs and the pits of my eyes. But to any who would come by I would proclaim the glory of the Lord and the imminence of the Savior he was sending to us.

"Are you an Essene?" they would ask. Or others, "Have you gone mad in the heat? Are you like Nebuchadnezzar of old who eats the wild things in his insanity?" But others heard my cries of repentance and heard the Lord, but with the wrong ears. "You must be Elijah," they would say. "You must be the prophet anew sent to save us from this exile." Did I have an answer to their questions? Did I know who I was or what I was doing in the wilderness? At times I did not, but when I had an audience I could not help but to cry out of my lonely stomach that the Day of the Lord was near. My people needed to know the time had come. Then he came to me. We were reunited.

My father never believed in Jesus. He told me this without veiled speech. But my mother did so fervently that her belief was in me as well. Had I not seen him do amazing things? Had I not heard his voice boom with the might of Sinai? Now, grown men, myself clothed in camel's hair, with a beard untamed by the wind, and he, dressed as a fisherman, with eyes as blue as his voice was deep. We had not seen or spoken in many years, it seemed, but the wilderness keeps few records of such things. A churning began in my gut as I identified my friend and my spirit rose within me. My mother's voice rang and chimed in my head and Messiah, Messiah, Messiah, all my hopes became this man.

"This is the one of whom I speak," I said to the small crowd that had gathered. "This is the man, the one who comes to baptize in fire. He comes with a winnowing fork in his right hand. He comes to clear the threshing floor and separate the Lord's people from the people of the powers of the earth who will be burned with a fire that cannot be quenched. This is the man sent from our Lord, of whom I am not worthy to touch his sandals."

And then he came to me and grabbed my hand and touched my face, speaking to me with the voice of a boy. "John, my friend, this is the way it was set by my Father to take place. Today you are to baptize me so that the will of the Lord may be made clear for all righteousness. It is well for you to do so."

I did not know what to make of his words but I was compelled to obey.

———————————

Thus began the ministry of Jesus. I began his false mission as Messiah. Soon after this day he disappeared for forty days. He knew the tradition. He knew the symbolic power of this number. A number of freedom, a number of new life, of transformation. But nothing changed. By the time he returned I had already been imprisoned for standing up against the sin of Herod. All great prophets are brave and speak out against the sin of the time in which they are sent. I had no choice but to tell Herod his incest with Herodias was despised by God. I had courage. The Messiah had come. I had proclaimed it. My time in the desert was not in vain. The Lord had allowed me to live in the time of his great redemption. Herod was not God. Herod would no longer act as God.

But when Jesus returned he was no Lion. He was a Lamb. Did he not realize what the times demanded? The Lord brings not an embrace but rather a sword, ready to cut down the nations that oppress his people. Instead, my disciples came to my cell to tell me of Jesus' ministry. Jesus says, "Blessed are the poor in spirit, for they shall inherit the Kingdom of Heaven. Blessed are the meek, the peacemakers, the merciful." Jesus teaches to "Give to Caesar what is Caesar's and to God what is God's." He speaks to the people telling them "they are salt and must not lose their saltiness, that they are lamps that must shine in darkness. He implores the people to "not be angry at those who persecute, but rather to love them and to turn the other cheek so that they might strike them once again."

These are easy words to speak on a hilltop. They broke my soul in this cell.

How could I have been so wrong in my mission? This boy I knew, how could he leave me in this prison if he is the Son of God they say he is? He speaks of freedom of the spirit and the reward for the fulfillment of those who hunger and thirst for righteousness, but what of his own friend who languishes in captivity for doing the work of a prophet of the Lord, the one he dares call Father? What of his baptizer?

My disciples were patient to hear my doubts. "Master, shall we go to Jesus and ask of him these questions? Shall we see if he has the words you need of him?"

"Yes, ask of Jesus this. Ask him if he is indeed the one who we have been hoping for or if we still must wait for another." I waited several weeks for them to return; worried he had won them over and had convinced them to leave me to my wonder. But they came back to me with his response.

"Master, Jesus says that he heals many, and gives sight to the blind, he gives hearing to the deaf, and cleanses the lepers. Master, he says he makes the lame walk and calls forth the dead from their graves."

"Yes, and what of these things? We have seen great workings in our midst before. What of the freedom of the people? What of the Messiah? What of my very own chains?"

"Master, all else he said was, 'Blessed is he who takes no offense in me.'"

That was the end. I knew it then. I told them to leave me and to go their own way. I thanked them for their short companionship and told them to leave me to my shackles, leave me to the will of Herod. There would be no Messiah this day. I would surely die not knowing of which way the path I prepared might lead.

Bring Me Water

You have nothing to draw with, and the well is deep.

John 4:11

"*W*hat did he say to you?"

"He is not a man you want to meet," the daughter said.

"That is what he said?"

"No, mother. He is not a man for you to know about."

At the well, the daughter met the man's eyes and her heart went aleep. It cried to her with a savage tongue, a bedroom tongue, an only secret language. She both did and did not know what it was saying, and to know this, as she did, was unraveling. A wet spool is all she felt.

"Sit down, dear," the mother said. "Your face has no color. Tell us simply what it was that the man said to you."

"He is possessed, but he seems to also know this, so it cannot be that he is."

"The man has a demon in him?"

"Many demons."

It is true, the man's eyes were purely refracted flames, and the man did know this, because his mind was made to know this. It was what his mind was intended to know. His tongue, though, often, was tempered. Paradox, this was his tool even as a child. He kindly spoke mostly words no one would understand, as paradox is a language of.

"We must call the leaders then," the mother explained to the filling kitchen, the family having felt the need in the first room. "If he has a demon, or many demons, the man must be dealt with. You could have been killed, or worse."

"He told me that I must die," she said, with want.

"That you must die? What are you saying to me?"

"I do not know, mother. Somehow I think he spoke it as if I were too late."

"This all cannot be. Do you feel yourself? Did he put his demons in you, do you think?"

"It does not feel so."

Not a demon. This man was not a man of demons, but he was not well. He went to the forbidden town that evening to draw himself water, this simple task, but then the woman was brought to him, alone.

The man was exhausted by his life. The things he wanted and the things he must not want. Rest he was refused, at all times, and he had no one to blame.

No one he dared to blame.

*

The girl, the young woman, the daughter woke up from a long sleep. Her mother was over her, worried, restless, wondering if her daughter would ever come back.

"Ah, good morning, dear. You feel better I believe?"

"No, I feel thirsty. And hungry."

"Yes, you fell asleep before our meal. Here, have some water and we can speak."

"I only want the water."

The man spent the morning in prayer, in asking, his morning ritual to separate the day from what he hoped and what he had to do.

"You know what is needed, and you know why this is so. But you, you alone, know that I am a man who does not know all, and today knows very little. Why that woman? Why did you give me that knowledge of her and the many men? Why is such other knowledge refused of me, if you tell me you want me to be wholly them? It is one of your very commandments, this very knowledge."

The man was not given these answers, but that is why he asked.

*

"Dear, we must speak of the well. You told me so little, and you were so pale. Think of me, daughter. Think of the things that I must think. Imagine how this is for your mother."

"For my mother!" the poor girl shrieked. "For my mother! For my mother this is not a thing. This is a thing for me," as she gulped all of the cup. "He told me I would never thirst again with what he gave to me, and here I am today, alive, with a thirst greater than I have ever known. There is only desert in me, mother, do you see? Only the waste of being left. For my mother!"

"Calm yourself, dear. Hear your words. You do not know what you are saying. I will call for the priest. He will know what we need."

With this the girl sat herself down into sleep on the floor, upright against a table leg.

The man would not sleep for many days.

*

In Jerusalem, a long way from the girl's home in Sychar, the man walked the streets with his friends and thought only of Samaria and all that would be forgotten once he was gone.

He also thought of how life can only be mistold.

*

"Oh, yes, my girl. It does matter. It very much does matter. That, indeed, is the very thing that matters at this moment. Do you understand?"

"What is he supposed to do about that. What can he do?"

"We are not now concerned with what he is supposed to do, or what he can or cannot do. What we are concerned about, at this time, is what you are commanded not to do. Do you understand, young one?"

"He is a Jew. That I do understand."

The girl hated the heat in her blood. She wanted to feel stupid or lied to, again. She wanted to feel small and weak and in great need. But ever since his voice, she felt more alive than was allowed by her own set of estimations, a constant cell level murmur that resembled a rag being wrung.

"So, then, what else is it that you need to know? Why am I here if you do have this understanding?" the priest asked her, looking out of his empty face with the stomach eyes of a hawk, swirling in some demented hunger, flying only to digest, only to make unnecessary room.

"He is a Jew, my girl. A Jew whose father is, or was, a Jew. Do you know anything of this man, of his father or of his mother? Are they pure?"

"If I do understand you, master, then it does matter so very little. Not at all, as you say?"

"Ah, yes. That is correct. A Jew is the beginning and the end of it. That is very right."

"Tell him of the demons!" her mother added from behind the corner of the next room. "Tell him of the man's many demons! Master, the man tried to kill her!"

The priest looked interested, and his face was sore from the urgent required emotion it was forced to find. There were many muscles in the priest that had become young and unfed from ill use.

"Demons, my girl? You did not mention the demons."

"No, if I had, my mother of the large ears would have no need to shout, now would she, my master?"

"I suppose no. So tell me then all about the possession of the man."

*

"Perhaps we should fish, master? We will need food soon, and the sea tends to calm you on some occasions."

"Yes, it does," the man said back to his good friend, a beloved one. "But I do not know if I am fit for the sea today."

"We can do the work, master. You should rest. Your eyes are very dark. Have you slept?"

"When have you ever seen the master sleep?" another asked. The thirteen of them walked, twelve huddled around the one who was slumped at the waist and the shoulders and the neck. Even his ears looked too heavy for his frame. He needed to pray and to be alone. But what he really was in need of was the woman and the well.

"Yes, let us go to the water," he said to his friends. "We will need to eat and the sea does calm me. But first, allow me a few minutes to ask of my father."

His friends prepared the lines and the net, tied down the sails, and greased the cracking corners of the deck. It was time for a new boat, but this was the boat the two brothers were called from, and no one wanted to see it go. The man found a fig tree and kneeled in the shade.

"Allow me to see her. This cannot be a wrong thing for me to ask, or to desire? Or, if it is, truly against your will that I do see her again, then please take her from my mind. You can do this. You can out of your love for me. I do have to believe that you do love me and that you do have this purpose for me, and that this life you are forcing me to live is for your good. But, please, answer to me. Give me some sign, anything is what I ask of you now. I cannot walk with this thirst. My very blood is parched and slowing. Minister to me, father. I cannot live forsaken forever. Your will is what I seek and I trust you to find, on earth and in your kingdom that is coming. May it be."

The man had a way of finding deaf ears.

*

The afternoon at the sea was full of honest and untidy conversation. The man smiled among his friends as they recalled the tiny man and the large tree, and then his belly warmed hot as stones in the oven when he remembered how much the little man had felt loved. So few of his father's children ever felt this created.

In the boat there was no talk of fig trees, broken tables, or thoughts of silver. In the boat there were fish and the knowing that soon no one would be hungry.

"Master," the beloved one said on the walk home, "what do you want us to do this night?"

The man walked without hearing.

"Master," the loud one echoed, "shall we go into town and speak at the Temple? You have not spoken to the Pharisees in several days? They may be fooled into thinking they have silenced you. Master?"

The man walked without thinking, his eyes newly disturbed sand. Circles. The man needed to drink and so his body took him to the town of the well, but that is not where his father led him.

The friends went to their homes and prayed that the Lord would keep their master safe.

*

"Yes, how can I help you?" the old woman asked at the door.

"I am thirsty, woman," the man said, feeling out of his clothes, cold, guilty.

"Well, come in then, young man, and let me give you some water."

Then, as sudden as death, the man's mind bit down hard into the woman and she felt like she had just woken from a terrible and already uncatchable dream.

"I need to speak to your daughter."

"You! Get out of my home! Your devils have no place in this house! Help!" the woman pleaded, and the small town was urupt, and there were lamps lit as fast as wind swiping through a large field, and animals speaking their language of coming quakes as if the scalp of the earth was coming off. The daughter lay in bed with a blunt and deep sleep.

"I will speak to her, but I wish to do it with your will."

"Out!" she cried as she slapped the right side of his mouth. "The priest will deal with you with the power of our God!"

"Yes, the priest. I will go to him," he said with his left eye only burning into her slack face.

*

"I have come to speak to you. Will you listen to me?"

The priest was never spoken to.

"I will have words with you, my son, but I am no audience

for men of your caliber. Do you know who I am?" the priest asked. He wondered, for only the briefest moment, what season it was. His mind, in a shudder, tossed itself back to days of youth when he chopped down dense wheat in the fields.

"I know you. I know all there is to know of you."

"That cannot be, my son, but if you know who I am then you know very well that my time is most valuable. What is it that you seek my counsel on, young man."

"You do not call me the names I should be called, priest. You do not call me the son. I am not an age. You need to speak wiser words if we are to speak."

"Son, I do not know who or what it is you are seeking, but I have many tasks this day, and I am willing to help you if I can, but you need to do your part and tell me what it is that is bothering you. It is clear to me that you have a great burden."

"Yes."

"Then speak to me. Tell me your name. Tell me what it is you want."

"I want to speak to the daughter of the old worried woman. The young woman who has the many men. I need to speak to her again. At the well, perhaps. But soon."

"You!"

"Yes."

"Who are you! What is your purpose here! You will not harm this town?"

"No. I will do no harm to the town. I am here for peace. I do not come with a sword, but only with a voice. I do not yell, as so many do, and I do not demand. I only ask, but few hear, and even less follow."

"Who is your father! Where do you come from!" The priest had grabbed his staff and held it in front of his chest. The man was not amused, but he was forced to think of a thin string held up against the crumbling mountain. He also thought of the woman weeks before who had only reached out one withered finger.

"You, priest, do not have the words from where I am from."

"You are a Jew, and I know your people's filthy tongue. You may speak to me in Aramaic, or in Greek. You may say what vile plans you may have with that girl in the tongue of the Romans, if you wish. I speak the dark Egypt as well. I have more tongues than you, I trust.

"You do not have the words."

"Tell me of you father."

"My father, as you are thinking, ran off when I was a child. My father was not ready for me to be his son, and he is forgiven."

"It was your demons that made your father go, was it not!. You are worse than a follower of the Hebrew Lord, you are a son of Gohenna. You are a child of what the Athenians call Hades, are you not!" The priest was now shaking his staff at the man, and the man stood with his hands behind his back, arrested, still, sturdy as a cauldron.

"I do not come from the Lord. You have spoken wisely."

"But many of your people believe that all of us come from the Lord. It is what Moses taught."

"I am not many, and I am not few, I am only a way. Where I come from is narrow, and where I go is light, but I am not of Moses, and I am not of the Lord. I only answer to my father."

"The devil!"

"No, but he and my father are very near one another, this is so. They must be, you see, if the world is to be."

"The devil wishes to destroy the world as you wish to destroy my town and that girl. You are a man of fire and death, it is clear to what my god as shown me. You are not going to prosper here, so out, out of here, and out of him and out of my town!"

The priest for the first time then knew he was going to die and had no idea what was to come.

"It is all right, old man. We all will taste this. This is not what we have to fear."

The priest's back was turning from a rod into a scythe.

"It is life that must fill us with your shaking now."

"Who are you?" the old man asked as he dropped his staff to the ground. "Are you Moses? Are you Elijah? It is said that one is coming, but can it be a Jew? Is it you?"

The man walked one long step and took the shivering man into his arms. He held him close, like a sheared lamb, and stroked his hair slowly.

"My son, do not be ashamed. Even I do not know all the answers you feel to ask. It is good of us not to know. The law tells us to know, but we do not because we can not. Do you understand?"

"I do not think that I do, master." The priest's body was heaving, sobbing, but his dying dry eyes would not permit.

"It is well that you do not, my son. Do not fear what is to come. No man knows. No man ought. It is our living that is at hand. We fail to love because we only fear. Do you have ears to hear this, old man?"

"Yes, master. I only wish I had not wasted my life. Why did you not come sooner?"

"I do not know. My father sends me. Only he knows."

"What will you do with the girl? Will you take her from her mother? Her mother would die without her. She is so precious to her."

"I do not know, priest. All I know is that I need to speak to her of this water."

*

"We are wasting time, master. It has been three days since you have roiled the leaders." The zealous one peered at the man, not in defiance, but with a will unlike any of the others the man had known.

"Time. Time?" the man asked himself. "How time can be known."

"Master, it is rare that I fully understand you, and that is my weakness, but now I need you to speak plainly to me, to us, for us. Rome has our leaders it its golden jaw. The Temple is defiled with their greed. Where have you gone? Where are you with scattered tables before you? Have you forgotten your mission?" The zealot now felt so clearly alone, because it was not in him to follow, as it was in the others. His loneliness came from his love for the man, and now he knew he could not allow himself to die without a fight.

"You are a man of truth," the man said as he placed a large hand on his friend's cheek, palm facing out, upside down, his wrist a circus. "You and I should no longer walk together, I fear, but I do not want you to leave us. I fear that I need you more now than ever. My Father tells me now that I must trust you. You are a man of direction, I hear."

"Yes, so let us now get to the Temple. Whitewashed tombs, my lord! A brood of vipers! Sons of Satan! Hear your own words, the words that are a furnace in me, the words I wish to follow."

"Yes, those words feel so far from me, but I trust they are of my Father, and so of me."

"Master?" the beloved one asked. "You look as you did when we came down from the mountain. You have the look of Sinai all over your face. I am worried, teacher. You need to rest before we go to see the Pharisees."

"It is too far to see, my love. I am too awake for those who are sleeping in the name of the Lord."

"Perhaps you should pray?"

"No. My Father does not want to hear my questions, today. Time, time is short. I must be known. I cannot go into the city like this. She will know me before I let them."

"You cannot be speaking of the woman at the well!" the zealot now had both of his hands on the man. The man's shoulders were so narrow and frail it felt like clapping to shake him so. "She is only a Samaritan whore! That is in truth all that girl is. You said as much to us, of your immediate vision of her and the many men. You want to minister to whores, here, here in our own town, here they are! Is that your mission, you fool? Your Father wants you to speak riddles to women with loose minds? This cannot be!"

"You are true. This is not of my Father. This is only of me. You and my Father are one, it seems. But I am one. No man can get to the Father but by his own way."

With that the man walked off, away from his friends, and away from the will of his Father.

So he believed.

*

"He has been here," the old woman groaned, holding the smiling head of the priest in her hands.

The Temple in Sychar was quite cold, as if there was a great trumpet at the door, calling down all the wretched breaths of God, the exhales of hunger and lust, of poverty and sloth, the unknown repudiations that arose from creating finite beings with a fork within. Should one feel guilty?

The soul being an experiment of wills.

*

"How long have you been here?
"I do not know."

"Have you come to see me?"

"I have come to tell you of my water."

"You speak to me, master, and I will listen."

"You should not call me this. I am only a man today, and every day from now until the end."

"Then speak."

No thing moved in the air or under the air.

"We must walk. We cannot stay at the well."

"There is a nearby vineyard. Can we speak there?"

"Yes."

The man and the woman walked together, aligned, at an or-dained distance, a span that must not be made closer so as not to burn, but must not be lengthened for lack of warmth.

"I often feel like this," the man said as he looked not into her eyes, but behind.

"Like what? You look feverish. You feel warm?"

"Like these vines. I feel as though I can speak to you plainly and that will not harm you. Is this so?"

"You will harm me. I have known this from the moment I heard the tremble in your voice and saw the pain in your eyes. But you must. Speak to me."

"I am here because my Father who is above the earth and above the kingdoms of the earth has sent me. He directs me, and he fills me with a thirst for the weak and the poor that few un-derstand. I rarely, do you see, know of my Father? It is not that I ever know, but I feel pulled like a mute, towards the casted off, and so that is how I am made to feel."

"We need great men to care for the lowly. Your Father is good to lead you towards them."

"My Father is many things, all things, and so he can not be any thing other than a crippling master. He does not know how to care for us, though I believe that it is in his will to do so, he has no way to."

"Perhaps that is why he sent you to us?"

"If I knew."

The man took in a deep breath and his lungs filled with ice that soon melted into usable air. The woman looked on him and saw a child with a frenzied mane. She wanted all there was of him, to know him, not the way a man knows a woman, but the way a woman knows a man. The way a woman can make a man's chest feel like a cage again.

"Let me tell you a story."

"Yes, tell me."

"I once was in the desert for a long time."

"Were you lost?"

"No."

"Did you have water? Why did you not leave?"

"I had no water and I could not leave. My Father wanted me to speak to his brother. I had to choose whom to love."

"And you chose your Father, of course?"

"It was not so simple, but yes, I think that I chose wisely. But his brother, you see, has not left me alone. His brother has won the love of so many I fear my love cannot be strong enough."

"Who follows his brother?"

"Your priest, for a time. Your mother. Herod knows him well. The wealthy men in my town. Even the man who loved my mother. Most who love the brother are not wrong to love him, because he is the only one who asked of their love. Man cannot only love himself, so he must learn to love my Father or his brother."

"Then why would not many follow your Father and not the brother? I do not understand."

"Because," the man said as he brought his finger down from her hair towards her nose, and then across the horizon of her lips, "my Father requires that we die before we can live.

The brother allows for abundance, for comfort, for days upon days of laughter and too much wine. My Father is the will of denial. The brother is far more accepting."

"Why? Tell me? Why is your Father this way?"

"Because he is responsible."

"And that is why he sent you? To teach against the brother?"

"I believe so, but now I see. I can not."

"Why?"

"That, woman, is why I am here with you. I must be known before I can know forward. You must tell me how I can love one and not the other."

*

It is said that the woman did know the man, and it is said that she did not. No one knows. Many things have been written of the man and of the Father and of the brother. The woman has been allowed to pass in the silence. Many have claimed to understand the man, to love the man, to follow the man, and many things have been done with a will that claims to be in the name of the man. What is known is that the man died as intended.

But who are you, oh man, to believe that My son's purpose is to be understood.

On an Old Saw

that is, that I may be encouraged together with you
while among you, each of us by the other's faith, both
yours and mine.

Romans 1:12

Setting is in the third heaven, where some have been caught up into. It is not so much an actual setting, but you will get the idea. It is more an idea than a place. Most places are, really. There are five men who are caught up into this idea at the moment, so to speak. One is always there.

J.

J is there with one of those beards that you just don't trust, because he really cannot pull it off, but he is still going for it. Like, give it up already, J. What is the point?

Paul is there for the third time and he is really excited to be. He used to be called Saul, but now he is Paul. He seems to think or believe maybe that he and J go way back, like they had some sorta moment or something. He is always rubbing his hind-end, though, as if he just got kicked by a jackasss or dropped from a very high place.

Fred *is there with his mustache. It is the first thing you notice about* Fred. *Not the only, but the first. He speaks as if instead of a throat box or whatever it is called, he has a sorta orchestra in there, all sown up, like a trumpet, at least, this voice.*

Soren *is there with wild hair and very child-like eyes, the kind of eyes you see, or look into, and say. "well, geez, those sure don't match his words or face." Like they were sorta put there by mistake and that is why they tremble when he speaks, you know?*

Jean *is there and he is old. Like real old, like bald why are you still around old. But his words are hot, always, and he looks around real quick and always. He seems like he wants to fight, but not real knock down drag out fight, like he wants to get in your head and screw around a bit. I say want to. I should say do.*

They are sitting in a circle. Sometimes Paul *stands up and walks around.* Soren *almost always stands or maybe always.* Fred *sits but the way he sits is almost like he is running.* Jean *sits pretty normal. J, though, it is really hard to say with J. He sits, yeah, but like, not floats, nothing spooky, more like he sits and the chair, well, no. He sits and you get the feeling, yeah, like a really strong sense that he could jump real high if he wanted to.*

So here it is.

<u>ACT ONE</u>

J: Many are called, but few chosen.

Soren: So true.

Jean: To be sure.

Fred: Here we are.

Paul: Boasting is necessary, though it is not profitable.

Fred: Jesus Christ.

Soren: Careful.

Fred: No, really already. This guy. With this? Boasting?

Soren: Careful only in the aesthetic sense... why are we here?

Fred: We are. Be grand.

Jean: No, be serious. Why are we here?

J: To die.

Fred: Now something real, something true.

Paul: Speak to me with truth.

Jean: We are getting at it.

Soren: Are we always here?

Jean: You may think so. Your ideas have always been here. So here you are.

Paul: But the time is short. We must speak the truth while there is still time.

Soren: Slow down. If we do not sleep that is time all the more. We should also stand.

Fred: You fools.

Jean: We are getting there.

Paul: I am becoming foolish. You yourselves compelled me. Actually, you should commend me. I am not inferior, even though I am nobody.

J: No. Not that.

Soren: You do not believe that anyone is, do you? No-body?

Paul: Some are.

Fred: Shall I thwack you now? You need a good thwacking. Nobody ever told you?

Jean: He is not much of a listener, I see.

J: Perhaps it is thirst.

Soren: Yes, he is. But without it we would not have need. Thirst is an angelic thing.

Fred: Shut up and get back to it. Words are what you use to execute your will. Execute!

Jean: You are mostly right.

Paul: Your will? You do not have a will except for that which is given to you.

At this point J rubs his wrists, like he is really itchy all of a sudden.

Jean: This doesn't make much sense in my time.

Soren: Nor mine.

Fred: No shit.

Paul: All times are a gift of grace, as this meeting is given to us from on High. He is here, do you not know this?

Soren: But you are talking of faith? Not knowing.

Paul: Faith is given to us from above.

Soren: Then what of us?

Paul: It is not about us. It is about our Lord Jesus Christ.

Fred: Jesus Christ, with this. You seem to believe it is very much about you.

Paul: Only in that I am a bondservant of Jesus Christ, called as an apostle, set apart for the gospel of God.

Fred: Do you hear this guy? I am almost ready to speak.

Jean: Do.

Soren: Yes.

Fred: Not yet. Let friend-o here lay it out for us. Okay, so a question.

Soren: He is not ready.

J puts his hands up toward the top of the place and says nothing.

Jean: The silence is correct.

Fred: With all this coming from above, what of our will? Lay it on thick. I need to get this first.

Paul: With pleasure.

Paul rolls up his sleeves.

Paul: The doctrine of our Lord Jesus Christ is simple to those who are willing to listen.

Fred: "Willing" – you all heard that premise. Noted. Go.

Paul: Please, allow me some time at length to explain and then I will listen. I am here to tell you all of the good news of Jesus Christ. All are guilty without the blood of the lamb, but the blood has been shed, so not all must perish. You see, the wrath of God is swift and just, and it is revealed from heaven against all ungodliness.

Jean: If I may, a question. Why are all guilty, as such?

Paul: This is simple. All are born of the sin of Eve. All are stained and must be washed clean by the blood of the lamb. We cannot will our way out of what has already been done.

Soren: But, it seems, without the ability to choose in the moment of crisis than faith is impossible? Faith is than nullified, sir?

Paul: Faith is given from above. We do not know who is chosen to be awakened to the truth of Jesus Christ, for only some are elected to have their will purified in the blood.

Jean: This is a frightening conception of human life, is it not? Yet you seem so comforted by it. Could it be, my new companion, that what frightens you is the possibility of human choice? That dreaded responsibility of consciousness?

Paul: I only fear not doing my duty by the Son of God. I am made in the image of God and must therefore bear what burdens he lays before me.

Jean: This outward imposition you desire must be something. It is my belief that man is only what he makes of himself. What else could he be?

Paul: A follower of the Christ.

Soren: I feel we are farther off than I first thought. It would be good to get some fresh air, maybe go to a play? It is great fun, to go, or to sit at a café and watch the churchgoers go by, and have them stare at you, condemned as you are, anathema! their eyes say, and my heart laughs as I know I am the one living for faith, and they so many objects of Constantine. A coup!

Fred: You forget where we are. We are stuck with this blowhard for as long as J here sees fit.

Paul: Your anger and bitterness are clear.

Fred: Is that right! At least I have the will to live. The will to take a hammer to the old gods, to the Church you built, the Church that is hostile to life and hostile to this earth. You think you are some messenger of God, or the Christ. You fool! *You made* the Christ! The Christ is in your damned head, and now, thanks to your guilty-ass broken heart, you murderess wretch, millions will die without ever having lived one god damned day! Anger and bitterness, it is only thanks to my grand style that I do not strangle you in front of this group right now, this very moment.

Fred catches his breath, runs both hands through his hair, stands up and looks to J.

Fred: It is only out of my respect for you, that I leave the room now, and promise to return.

Soren: Perhaps I should follow him. He does not seem well, and being alone can really get to a man.

Soren walks off to find Fred. J goes to the corner of the room, backed turned to the circle, and kneels.

Paul: Not all have the ears to hear the words of above. I am glad you are still willing to hear.

Jean: I am willing to speak with you. I feel a very deep responsibility to speak with you and to try to understand one another. Do you wish to understand one another, or is your heart only intend upon what you think of as preaching the good news?

Paul: I have been called and shackled to the Gospel.

Jean: Yes, I see. Than may I ask you a question?

Paul: Yes.

Jean: Is it fair for me to assume that you would be greatly distressed if I were to tell you that God no longer exists? That in your time he may have, and may have even died on the cross, but that in my time, God no longer is with us?

Paul: That is blasphemy! God always was and always will be.

Jean: I see. And you know this?

Paul: As sure as I know I am Paul, the apostle of Jesus Christ.

Jean: But were you not also the tent-maker from Tarsus?

Paul: This is true.

Jean: And were you not also a great slayer of those who followed "the lamb," as you like to say?

Paul: I am a new man now.

Jean: Yes, we see. That is what I am offering to you as a premise, if nothing else. We are a part of a new man as well, a man who no longer has God to trust or fear, and this is greatly distressing for us, you see. We are not happy about this. We do not celebrate the loss of God. There is no glee here. But we do see that we are no longer able, us new man, to have the certainty that men like you once had. Our faith exists because of our great unknowns.

Paul: Than you have no faith.

Jean: I see. It is odd, it seems, that you and I can both be so anguished, but so very unable to understand one another. I wish we could communicate. Here, let me ask another question. What is it that anguish means to you?

Paul: Anguish? Anguish is merely a product of the flesh. The spirit must live within the flesh, but the flesh is weak, and the spirit must overcome it. Anguish is living in a world where darkness rules, where there is so little light. Anguish is waiting on the Lord to come back and end this sickness that the sinfulness of man has begotten, this rotting world. Anguish, anguish is this thorn in my side, this constant agony in my inner man. I pray and pray for God to relieve me of it, but still I do not find relief.

Jean: We are not so far off.

Paul: What is anguish to you?

Jean: A question! Delightful. I was nearing a state of forlorn. Anguish, anguish to me. It is what a teacher of mine once called the "anguish of Abraham," you see. I know that you know the story. God, or an angel of God, calls Abe and says, "Abe, I know you have waited all this time for this son of yours. I know I really put you through the wringer on that one. But Abe, here's the thing. You really now have to go and walk him up real slow up a mountain and then take your knife from your belt and hold that little boy's neck to a stone, and you need to slice his throat until you watch all his blood leave him. Can you do that for me, Abe?"

Paul: It was a test of faith.

Jean: Oh, without doubt. But here is the anguish. If Abe could *know* that the essence or thing or person that was speaking to him, commanding him, was *really* the Creator of the Universe, the One and Only, then it would be a tough thing to kill your son, but extremely doable. The anguish comes in with the questions that must be asked – Is it really an angel, or could it be a demon? Is he really speaking to me? Who am I? Am I? What proof do I have of any of it? How do I really know that I am in fact Abe? And then, based on that flimflam of consciousness, he must will himself to an action, and that action will define him, in that eternal moment, forever.

Paul: I do not believe in those questions.

Jean: You cannot. They are not to be *believed in*. You are too much stuck in the either/or of nonbeing. Some say we must act based upon a universal notion, you see. I will do this or that because if everyone acted as I am planning on acting than the world would be a better place. But then that man must ask of himself, "Am I really the kind of man who has the right to act in such a way that humanity must guide itself by my actions?" And if he does not ask himself that, he is masking his anguish, and if anguished is masked or side-stepped, than so is life.

Paul: I believe we all must act as Jesus Christ acted, that we must believe on the Lord, be justified by faith, and therefore will find peace with God through the blood of Jesus Christ.

Jean: Than why are you here?

ACT TWO

Well, that was something.

J is still in the room. He refuses to leave this idea. It would feel to J, I think, and this really is just my surmisal or whatnot, but leaving this room would feel to J something like leaving your own skin. Most of us have been there, and it is no place to be. I think, and again, what do I know, but I think it would be good for J to take a breather.

Paul is ready to get back to it. This feels like a buffeting for him. He is big into races and competitions and marksmanship and finishing the course and whatnot. His forearms are really big, one more than the other, and his neck, god, this guy has a neck on him. I bet, just as a guess, that he was a bear when he was young. What he needs, this guy, is sorta like a perpetual punching bag or something. He was made to be a boxer.

Soren is excited to get back to the group, but he lacks something, it seems. Like, he is not so much into the thin, or is not sure what the thing is. He does not see this so much as a place for winners and losers. He wrings his hands as he waits and listens, but not like he is nervous, more like he thinks a homerun is bound to fall into his lap soon. He is like the kid who brings his glove to the game, even though he is sitting in the 3rd deck, 600 feet from home plate, and sits there every night, and has never even got a sniff of those sizzling laces. But Dad promised a ball one day. But who is to say.

Jean is a bit beat. A bit worn out. But he is still in, and glad to be. He is the kind of old guy who has what some call something like old man strength. It is clear, to me at least, hard to say for anyone else, that he was a real ass-kicker when he was young, but never knew how. Or cared to. He spends most of the intermission looking up. Some look up when they lie. Some when they are sad. Some when they are asking. Some confused. But Jean *is none of this. He likes up. Or is it here.*

Fred *is a mess. He must have found some trouble out of the conversation. He wears the same plain white shirt he was wearing previously, but now, in red, it reads, "Festival Time!" I have no idea, I can promise you, what his handwriting looks like, but I feel as if, for some reason, this most certainly is not his own. It seems to be in the hand of a child. His mustache, already very much three ring in its own right, is on fire. No, no flames. But it looks as if it is smoking, writhing upward. He also is smoking and has brought a pipe that apparently he thinks* Jean *has asked for. He also has a rose for* Paul. *He is nibbling on one of its thorns.*

Everyone is back in the room, now. They all have assumed their previous seats.

J *has brought refreshments. He looks starved.*

Fred *pulls out a large goblet from his pocket. No one understands how.*

Paul *refuses both food and drink.*

Soren *asks* J *how much is right.* Jean *pours himself a glass, and sits back down, quietly.*

Fred: See, J, I told ya I would come back.

    J *smiles as he points at Fred's shirt.*

Fred: What, this? You like this? Ya, just something I came up with out there in the Great Beyond. Had some time to do some thinking and scribbling and then it felt like a man could sure use some festival time, some good old windbagging – Ye-A!

Paul: We are in sacred space here, you fool.

Fred: Oh, you. Welcome back. You two old saws get everything cut up nice and neat, I assume. Get your mental stretches all accomplished, did ya?

Jean: We did not quite even get to the Old Saw yet, but we are further along than when we began. Our friend here even asked a question.

Fred: Whoohee, there. And can a Festival man hear?

Jean: He asked me what I thought of anguish.

Fred: And you said, listening to your priestly idolatries, right! And you said, you call yourself a free spirit, free in the crucifixion of the Christ. You said, you feel you are dead in sin but alive in the blood of the lamb, alive to God in the death of the Christ. You said?

Jean: I remember being so young as you.

Fred: Okay, I will take a breath. Would you please tell me what you said to our man here?

Jean: We were beginning to talk about the burden of human choice. The responsibility of our freedom.

Fred: Aha – Ye-A! A little brave nonsense, some divine service and ass festival, some joy-full old super being fool, a blustering wind to blow your souls bright!

Soren: Is everyone happy?

J puts his hand on Soren's shoulder.

Paul: Your foolish words are a great tribulation to us. But we exult in our tribulations, knowing that tribulations brings about perseverance.

Fred: You are fortunate, friend of my friend, that I am in Festival attire.

Paul: Christ died for you, and this is how you repay him.

Fred: You killed Jesus!

Soren: No!

Jean: Let him say what he means.

Paul: It is true, I was a great persecutor of the faith.

Fred: You ass. The idea! You and your Christ! You do, tell me at least that you do, you do know that you *made* the Christ? Do you?

J wipes his brow, and quickly wipes his hand on the back of his shirt.

Paul: I am merely a messenger, a bondservant of our Lord.

Jean: Tell it another way.

Fred: We all in this room, god I want to, we all in this room know that friend-o here created out of a crucifixion an idea, a Christ, and then a life's calling, a mission for himself, a way of being in the world, and we all know he thinks it is a way of being for all the world, and we all know only a buzzard flies around their whole life over such a deathly way to be, and we all know this – *drinks deeply from a glass that seems to be growing* – we all know he does not belong at our festival of God's woe, his deep and everlasting woe, our festival to sing of this strange world, our festival to reach out to the woe of being, to reach out to God's woe for making it so. What am I? An intoxicated song, a sweet lyre, but not liar like the sainted one here, not a certain fool, a chosen fool, a willed fool, a foolish hammer – a midnight lyre, a croaking bell which no one understands but which has to speak before deaf people – you, saint bag, you Higher Man – it is your height, your up-ness, this is why you do not understand me. Gone, Gone, my youth. Oh Noontide. Oh afternoon! Now come evening and midnight; the dog howls, the wind, but is the wind not a dog? It whines, it yelps, it howls. Ah, now it sighs, how it now laughs, how it rasps and gasps the midnight hour. How it now speak so soberly, this intoxicated poet. Perhaps it has overdrunk its drunkenness or perhaps it has grown overwakeful or perhaps it ruminates? It ruminates upon its woe in dreams, the ancient, the deep midnight hour, and still more upon its joy, for joy, though woe be deep: joy is deeper than the heart's agony.

J and Soren break into applause.

Jean: Now we hit it.

Paul: He attempts to confuse and to be beside the point. It is simple, the wages of sin is death, but the free gift of God is eternal life in Christ Jesus our Lord.

J: No.

Paul: No? How can you say no?

J leaves the room.

Fred: See what you have done, pally? Do you see? Do you need another road to be knocked to? I have many blinding lights I could provide.

Paul: I thought he was the one. Where am I?

Jean: The first question you must answer is not that.

Paul drinks from his glass.

Paul: What is it?

Jean: Are you.

Paul: I feel I can say yes.

Jean: Good. Now, what are you.

Paul: A man, a bondservant of Christ Jesus.

Jean: Good, why are you.

Paul: Because of the perfect will of God the Father of Christ Jesus. Because of God's perfect will, his calling of me to serve his eternal purpose.

Fred: Yikes! And I thought I had it rough.

Jean: And who chose this to be so?

Paul: God, the Father. His divine will – it is he who chooses and he who elects. I am only a man, a bondservant.

Jean: May I try to teach you another way.

Paul: Where did J go?

Fred: I can tell you. He went into the Great Beyond, where I came in from to begin my festival. If you follow, you will also be in the Great Beyond and you will taste of the joy and will not be a thirsty skin. All joy wants is the eternity of all things, to go beyond good and evil, to swim and thrash in the cumulous ballooning of the opposites, to be filled and be felled by the great hot air of the other than the two of things, it wants love, it wants hatred, it is superabundant, it gives, it throws away, begs for someone to take it, thanks him who takes, it would like to be hated, so rich is this joy in the Great Beyond that it thirsts for woe, for Hell, for hatred, for shame, for the lame, for the world, for it knows, oh it knows the world – and you, you High Man, joy longs for you, joy the intractable, joy the bliss-filled, for your woe and your sick constitution, your wretched inner man, your homicidal past, your history bloodied dogmas, joy wants itself, therefore it also wants the heart of agony. Oh break, this heart. You, High man, learn of joy, learn this, learn that joy wants eternity, joy wants the eternity of all things, wants deep deep deep eternity. Have you learned of my song? Have you divined what it means? Very well, then, come on, you High Man, now sing our roundelay! The world is deep, deeper than day can comprehend!

Fred drinks the last of his cup, drops it, it shatters, and he passes out. Falls like rice from a burlap sack. Soren begins to cry slowly, and as he grabs Fred by the ankles to pull him out of the room, he is sobbing, heaving, gut level crying that pains the listener to hear. When you hear this, it feels something like it feels when you are in a theater and there is a very explicit and in poor taste sex scene, and you remember when you walked in to take your seat and enjoy the show, seeing more than one family behind bulbous buckets of popped corn, with very young children. That wallet feeling you get, that anger too, like you want to rush up there and dump meaningless pieces of paper all over the Father and say something like, Goddamn you! Take this and get them a goddamn baby sitter already! What in God's name are they doing here!

So now Jean and Paul are alone.

Jean: What did you make of all of that.

Paul: I am thankful to be alone with you again.

Jean: What did you make of all of that.

Paul: We cannot go beyond good and evil, can we?

Jean: We can but should we.

Paul: I have to think that we should not.

ACT THREE

Sad to see. I was hoping, although I do not know if I am even allowed to hope in my role here, but I was hoping Fred *would stick around some. Some more, I mean.*

Who knows though.

Now before I set the scene of what I see here and now – I really do wish, and who knows now that I think of it if I am allowed to wish, at that – wish that you, whoever you might be, could see this all from my point of view, for lack of a better string.

Soren, just so you know, when he grows up, writes of this notion. Quite well, if I may.

But before I begin again, I would like to ask, because I do not know what is allowed, but that is the thing, who is it or what is it that would allow me to do or not do in the first place, or in any place? I understand that you cannot answer at this time. Trouble is, or in any time.

I do know that I am not allowed to take sides, here, and that is something I know because it is myself that will not allow me to do such a thing. It is just not just.

I was hoping, when I signed up for this, this role of mine, that it would make me a better man.

But is this all rabble? Where the rabble also drinks all wells are poisoned.

I think I must choose a side here, but I also know I must not. I must choose myself, to do the role I myself signed up for. But in choosing myself, I also choose all men. That rubs here.

I do feel older. And newer, too. I feel now acquainted with the needs of this life.

Don't you wish you had Fred *in your backyard, like a sorta wind chime you could now and again bash with a stick and make it yawp. I do. But then I would not want to break it, either. Or, maybe just his goblet? But I shall never again drink of the fruit of the vine until that day.*

Okay, now time for brass tax. Time I get back to work here. You all are waiting. It is time to get this undertaking underway.

It is simple. We only have Jean *and* Paul *left to hear.* Jean *is holding the rose* Fred *forgot to give to* Paul, *and he is twirling it in his hand as if his wrist were the beginning of a pinwheel.* Paul *is holding his glass between the palms of his hands and spinning it back and forth in short half turns, because he does not want the glass to turn completely around. The veins in his hands are very apparent, if you are up close, and it looks as if he is ready to smash the glass and brush the hair from the glass' eye at once.*

From the distance we hear nails being hammered and wood being sawed.

Jean *smokes the pipe* Fred *brought for him from the Great Beyond.*

Jean: Tell me why you are frightened.

Paul: Forgive me, but I truly forget why it is you think I am frightened.

Jean: No, forgive me then, my friend. I gathered from your need to believe that you were quite afraid. You may not be. This is true.

Paul: All men have fears in this world.

Jean: Oh, yes. God, yes. Vast anxiety. Anguish, as we put it earlier. Most of life is made up of these fears, or not. It does not have to be.

Paul: What are you afraid of?

Jean: Do you really want to know, or are you setting the mark for a polemic? Because, to be honest with you, you are a young man and I am not, and I am, I fear, a bit too weary for any more speaking for the pure sake of rhetoric. I would like to get at something, and then sleep.

Paul: No, I truly do.

Jean: I am afraid that my work will go unappreciated.

Paul: What is your work?

Jean: I am a philosopher –a speaker – a writer of plays and such. In short, I am a man who lives in ideas. Ha! I just thought of an actual Truth! So rare! Ha, yes. My friend, can I share with you an actual Truth!

Paul: Please.

Jean: I have no skills!

Paul: Surely you do.

Jean: Truly, it is true. Verily verily and all the rest. It has been struck. How freeing! I have no skills. Nothing to offer the world of things.

Paul: But you offer your words.

Jean: Yes. And what a treasure. But you see therein lies the fear. If all I have to offer the world are my ideas, my books, my speeches, and if they are not appreciated as I think they ought to be, or as they ought to be, who is to say, then I am living in a great deal of anguish. And for nothing. Perhaps that is the case in any case.

Paul: We share this fear.

Jean: How so?

Paul: I am also a writer and a speaker. A man of ideas. I was a tent maker, as you noted, but I am now a man who thinks. And I am afraid, because of my bond to Christ Jesus, that I will not run the race properly, that I will not offer the world what I have been called to offer the world.

Jean: If I may?

Paul: Please.

Jean: Your words will be much appreciated.

Paul: That is kind of you to say.

Jean: Friend, you do not understand?

Paul: Understand what?

Jean: My dear man, I *know* this. I am not flattering a guess. You do not know where we are?

Paul: A sort of vision, I take it. In the house of the Lamb.

Jean: How can I tell you of this and not cause you to leave me. Paul, I can look back and see you, but you cannot look forward and see me, time being what it is. Being, time, etc.

Imagine Paul's face at this one, huh? Well, it is quite ridged up and ruffled. Jesus, what if someone told you such a thing.

Paul: You are saying this is real?

Jean: As real as it can be.

Paul: And you are saying you are from the future?

Jean: Well, I am saying you and I are fortunate enough to be allowed to be here where past and future are no things and we can truly speak in the moment. It is terribly rare.

Paul: So is that why Fred hated me? He knows what became of my life and he hates it?

Jean: Aha. I meant to ask you again what you made of all of that.

Paul: Tell me.

Jean: It is a difficult thing to tell.

Jean fills their two glasses from an old wine bag of J's that has been sitting on a table far left.

Jean: Fred is a man much like you and I, or he was for a time. He and I do not share a time, but we are much closer than you and I, in that sense. Would you truly like me to tell you of him and attempt an explanation? I must warn you, before you answer, that he is not necessarily an explainable occurrence in the world.

Paul: Why does he hate me?

Jean: He thinks you killed Jesus. He said as much.

Paul: But what a fool he is! I had nothing to do with the murder of the Christ, although all of us are guilty for his death because of our sins.

Jean: Now we hit it.

Paul: He hates me because I killed Jesus. How can this be?

Jean: He hates that you believe in salvation. That is as simple as I can tell it to you. You must realize, my new friend, that the man wrote a whole book against you. It is one of the most known books of our world, in terms of the world of ideas.

Paul: The fiend! How dare he, that crazed son of Satan has the nerve to write against Paul, called an apostle, a bondservant of the Creator!

Jean: Ah, see.

Paul: I am sorry. But I am growing to hate that man. I do not mean to boast.

Jean: He is gone now. No need to worry. But tell me, why do you believe in salvation? Is it because you fear what is next, after life, as you might say? What is to come?

Paul: Well, yes. I fear going to Hell, as any man does. I do not want to be one of those damned souls who do not confess in the name of the Lord, who spend eternity in the brimstone of the Fallen One. Who would?

Jean: Who?

Paul: Who would choose Hell?

Jean: Ah, I meant who is this Fallen One?

Paul: Satan, the fallen angel of the Lord. The serpent of old who tricked the first woman to eat of the fruit and thus stain all of mankind with the sin of the Fall. Satan, the great enemy of the Lord Jesus Christ, the Great Tempter, the Beast, the one who wishes for all of God's creation to suffer with him in Hell for all of time.

Jean: Oh, him.

Paul: So you do know of him?

Jean: Yes. I learned most about him from you.

Paul: Then why did you ask me?

Jean: Paul, I was truly hoping things had changed.

There now is a sound from far off, a great creaking, as if a large awful thing is being pulled up against its own will.

Now a hammering, again, but this time so hollow the noise, that it sounds like knocking.

Jean: Allow me to speak at some length, if you will? I am an old man, I am sure you have noticed? Ha, yes, you must have. I do not have the strength that you still possess and the time is nearing when I will need to rest. But here it is as I see it? May I?

Paul: Yes, you may, my friend.

Jean: You are a man who has a vibrant mind, but a mind that operates in the either/or of things. You think of the world, or when you look onto the world, you see good and evil. You see light and darkness. You see chosen and lost. You see saved and damned. You see followers of what you call the Christ, and followers of what you think of as Satan. This is what I gather from your work, and I do think that I know your work well, and you may at any time please correct me when I get afar from how you understand yourself.

Paul: But I do not see the trouble with that. And you do have it correct.

Jean: The trouble is what goes back to what Fred was trying to convey about the thrashing of the opposites. You see, we have come to see the world as neither either or or, as not one or the other, because of the fact that there is not God to define for us what it is to be us. And I know, I know even me simply saying that string of words, "there is not God" makes your very arm hair boil, your neck bones revolt, your tiniest of toes stand at attention, but effort to listen still. If there is not God, and there is only man, and there is only the world that we live in inside our own temporary skin, then the world is a much different place than your idea of this or that, good or evil. It is a world of existing in the beyond of experience itself. It is an awful and essential way to be. So, when you came along and spoke and wrote of the

Christ and how it is his death and his blood that humanity needed to be saved from their sins, and it was confessing in this name
of yours that would save humanity from this world, from this
wretched place of evil, and it was this confession that would pull
humanity out of this sick world and up into a world of good, a
world of peace, a world of light and harmony, men like Fred and
myself, well, we are in our own way very much fearful of such
teaching. In large part, it pains me to say, especially now that we
know one another as we do, we are fearful because we have seen
very clearly what havoc such either/or thinking can create in our
world.

Paul: Do not tell me. I cannot hear this.

Jean: I know. The rest is not for me to say.

> *The knocking is louder now, and the creaking. But now the creak-
> ing is like a door the size of a grand castle draw bridge being opened.
> Before we know it, J is in the room.*

> *J walks over to Jean and reaches out his hand. Jean stands up,
> knees cracking, and shakes the hand.*

J: I appreciate the time you spent here, son.

Jean: It was my great pleasure.

> *Jean takes a few steps to where Paul is sitting, hands him the rose,
> and places both of his hands on the man's broad shoulders.*

Jean: You are not a bad man. Guilt is another thing all together.

Paul: I hope to see you again.

Jean smiles and walks off.

J: The time has come.

Paul: What am I to do, master?

J: Begin by not thinking of me as master. You will be back here again. For now you need to rest. Your burden is breaking my heart.

Paul: Where do I go? Why do I go? What is my mission?

J: None of us are allowed to know. One day you will see. To know would ruin the whole point of going.

Paul: I want you to know, I still believe in you with all of my heart. I will die confessing your name.

J: I understand. I wish you peace, in time, on your journey.

Paul kneels before J, and gives him the rose. Walks away with his head low.

J takes the wine skin and pours himself a glass. The wineskin is taut, now, and J runs a finger around the perimeter. He is humming a tune that is droll, yet soothing. He looks toward the Great Beyond, pulls his free hand through his hair, and sighs. Then he looks out.

J: Those who are outside get everything in parables, in order that while seeing all of this, they will not perceive, and while hearing, they will not understand. Otherwise, if all understood the mysteries, there would be no reason to know. Do you not understand? Do you understand all of the parables? The sower sows the word. And these are the ones who are beside the road where the words are sown, and when they hear, the words are immediately snatched up and away. Those who are on the rocky places hear the word and receive great joy, but their joy is fleeting, because it can take no root in the word. They have no firm root in themselves. Affliction feels like punishment to them. They want to receive benefit for doing good, and be scolded by the world for doing bad, but this is the world of children, not the world of the word. And others will hear the word amongst thorns, and they do hear of it, but the worries of the world, and the business of men, and the noise, the efficient humdrum, the ever impressing need to feel you are progressing, or among those who are, that rushing liquid force of human greed, these are the thorns that will choke out the seed of the word so that the real will not be sown. The word bears no fruit. And some have the good soil, and they will hear of the word and accept it, and it will bear much fruit – an investment that will clear the eye of a needle.

Soren is standing behind J. He is dirty.

Soren: I do not understand you. I never have.

J: Why do you think you should?

Soren: My father. My father beat us until we could memorize your words. My father made us confess your name, the eternal name of the spotless lamb. My brother lost his mind over you. I fear I am in for the same fate. What I saw out there was no help, as I know you know.

J: How is Fred?

Soren: Resting, again.

J: How are you?

Soren: In need. In great need. Can you help me?

J: The seed sprouts and grows, but how, no man can know.

Soren: Explain yourself to me! I want to believe again. What of your words are to be taken seriously? In all the good news I find so much to be worried over. In all your kingdom speak I find so much to be nonsense. In all your actions I find so much to be impossible to follow. In all the doctrine in your name I find so much to be hateful. In all the off-shoots of your life I find so much to be rotten. In all my musings on you, my writings in you, my obsessions of you, I find so much to be robbing me of my life. Help me, please. Help me know what to believe?

J: Son, I am not to be believed in. In this life, or in your life, the important thing is not believing in the correct person, or thing. The path you follow, the bliss you seek, the journey you take, the living you do, the pain you survive, the mistakes you accept, the folly you find humor in, the deaths you avoid causing, the death you finally find – these are the reasons to continue to be. Not a belief. Not a position. Not a decree.

Soren: Are you God? Are you fully God? Are you man? Are you fully man? I am weary, so weary of paradox, of paddling out over those waves, of thinking. Why can't I be like the jiggly Danes who go about the streets on a Sunday afternoon with a heart full of heaven and hands full of pluffed sugar whip, eating and licking their lips, laughing at the gossip of the day, eagerly expecting the evening meal?

J: You ask because you do not have, and I do not have what you seek. But you have already discovered so much, you know how much of the infinite resides in you. Embrace it. Allow them to be diluted in thoughts of the infinite, while you are able to reside in the infinite. Allow them to enjoy sugar while you enjoy the very heat of the stars and circular moons of your mind. Allow them to live an emperor's day, while men like you ride on the back of the leopard through the mad rush of a condemned man's night. You, my son, must embrace the grand unknowable moment, and leave your father behind. I know what following the dreams of a father can do to a young man's path, and you have a narrow and lonely road to walk, a road no other man is fit to walk, so go and have the will to walk.

Soren: You ask so much of me.

J: You are asking it of yourself.

Soren: And I must go it alone?

J: There is no choice.

Soren: Will you watch over me?

J: I have no say. But I will think of you often, and when I am lonely, I will be lonely with you.

Soren: I do not feel ready to go back out there yet.

J: We never can feel ready for the tectonics of our living. One day you will look back and see the path you have walked, and it will now look like a path, but as you are walking, always peering to find the path, always certain that you have gone a foul way, wanting to retrace but knowing the road back is too far, wanting to call out for help, but fearing you will be heard by monsters and not a friend, feeling the load on your back is too stern, wishing you were a lion and not a camel, feeling your knees rupture like olives in the beak of a crow, wanting nothing more than to know where you are going and when you will get there. Just trust me that once you get there you will wish you were back on the path-less path. Once you let go of your load, your back will groan. Life cannot be lived in the wrong direction.

Soren: Life is lived forwards, but understood backwards. This is what you are telling me.

J: This means you are ready to get to it. Now you are in business.

Soren *hugs* J *fiercely.* J *puts his hands in* Soren's *wavy hair and makes it into a wild nest and both men share a laugh as* Soren *exits out into the Unknown.*

J *then kneels and begins to trace on the ground with one finger. What appear to be concentric circles. Humming his tune. Modeling amen.*

After These Things

Blessed is he who reads and those who hear
the words of the prophecy, and heed the things that
are written in it; for the time is near.

Revelation 1:3

"Fire of Jerusalem alive now burns then." This is how my master's notes from Patmos begin. "After these things we eat grace of meat and blood of grace." That is how his notes end, but there is much to read and contemplate of the in between – his rantings and the ravages of his mind, but also his memories and his faith, his clarity and his darkness. All of these found a way into his notes that I have been charged to now make into an Apocalypse to the churches – a revelation from our Lord of what is to come of us. But before I can attempt this awful task, I must transcribe his notes, for myself, or for someone who might find my own notes, once I too am gone and no longer under the cloak of the fathers. I must put his thoughts before my own and out of their sight before I write his book. I do this for the sake of the Church by the will of the Father, through the grace of our Lord Jesus Christ. Amen.

Fire of Jerusalem alive now burns then. Cities once city bear witness to flames. The flames on high on dragon high – winged flames of the city down. The once city now low and dragon high – proud flames of horns the dragon high fires pieces of the gone city low coal. No more.

*

I have read these wild words of dragons this morning as I sit in my cave and do not know what hand has written them. I awoke to the morning waves, the sometimes hiss and other times snap of the morning sea, and here find notes. I had until now thought I was alone on Patmos, but this is not my writing – surely not my words. What am I to make of it? I have spent the morning praying to the Lord, asking for peace from this trouble. I can only add to these dragon thoughts my own memory of the city that was taken from us almost thirty years ago.

The war began a generation after the Jews, my once kinsman, killed our Lord. Christ had been dead exactly as many years as he had lived when the insurrection began. I was a leader. We fought against Rome with the same might with which we loved our risen Lord. But our strength was no match for the powers of the earth in combat. In a few years time all our world was in ruins. Our land was renamed, Jerusalem and Masada had fallen, and those of us who survived had to live under the frightful and thin veil the churches provided. My eleven fellow disciples had been martyred and I both hoped and feared I would face the same end. But I was indeed the most beloved of the Lord's disciples. I had faith I would be exalted according to His good time and pleasure. When the Roman guards found me in Ephesus my life was spared. I was sent to this island as an exile, and here I have been waiting patiently for the Lord to reveal his will to me. But this morning I find the scrawling of a mad man next to my bed. I am restless and must find my morning meal.

A new day and no notes. I still feel unfit for prayer as my heart races against my mind. The day is hot and very young. The shade of my cave is weak. I am weak. There have been no fish for days. I do not know how long it has been since I have heard the voice of another man. I am growing sick of my own voice. I do not know what to recognize as my own at times. I hear gulls squawk away entire days and the dullness of the water is a constant pull on my own tides. When I find myself nodding from hunger I think of His breast. The Lord. My resting at the last table. I try to taste the bread, but I am only made of salt now. My lips and tongue are white slabs of salt. I am thick and unfit.

*

Behold the trumpet door and doors of thrones. The numbers to hold behold below. The throne of jasper behold below and hear the trumpet door, the lions roar behold. Hold the seals of jasper throne – see the eyes of jasper of the lions door and behold what they can hold. The number is four to behold. Holy you who behold must be below the holy one cry out from down low what you behold. How many eyes are low? You are old. Twenty four are old.

*

I fear these words. I fear these words are my words. Why can I not remember these words? Oh Lord, how long must I fear these words? How long, Lord? How long? Reveal to me your words, Oh Lord. I do not wish for any other. Amen.

*

There is heaven and earth and below the earth. There is weeping and heaven and earth and below the earth. Who is worthy in heaven and earth and below the earth? Some are slain and some between and some are sealed and slain and between. Does the Lion know the Lamb? Call the Lamb and see if the Lion will lay with the slain between heaven and earth and below the earth. Place the Lamb and the Lion below the throne. Open the seals and behold what is below.

*

I no longer only awake in the morning. It seems I am always coming awake. At times I awake on the beach in the wretched heat and stink of midday. Other times I will be on top of one of the monstrous crags that climb out of the sand. I am always hungry and I have no recollection of eating. I pray. I pray to the Lord to reveal himself to me. Then I awake and find notes if I am in my cave or large words dug around me in the sand. SEAL. ROOT. LAMB. LAMB. On the crags there are leaves and plant shoots arranged as images of cats and birds and cows and men. I am not alone. I am empty of strength and appetite.

*

I am the Revelator! The Lord in His goodness and grace has revealed Himself to me at long last. All my tremors and fear were part of His plan. These notes I have been finding, these images – all will be made known. The Lord has told me to wait for him and that all will be made known. I am to be the vessel of the Revelation of the Lord to his churches. I am to tell the world of its end. I am still his most Beloved. He was the one with me on the island – the one in whom I place my trust. All will be made known.

*

Worthy to be slain and felled, fell forever down the fallen and slain who fell. Slay the seals and fall down worthy to be slain. The red horse has fell. Conquer and come all you worthy and red. Take peace and slay another the one who fell. Seven you must break and fell. The creatures voice is red and worthy

– behold what the creatures tell those who felled the Lamb – behold the slain – the red creatures. Jerusalem fell. Those who dwell on earth are felled. The sword and the slain of the worthy that fell forever down.

*

I am no longer afraid of these words for the Lord is with me and has promised me visions. More visions. The Lord is blessing and keeping me and that is why I am always awaking. I cannot be awake and see what the Lord will have me see. As Moses was taken to the great mountain and walked with eyes sheathed on the ground of the holy so must I be taken up to the Lord with my mortal eyes closed and when I wake, fully, once all of the visions have been made known, then these notes will be revealed to me and to the people of the earth. I am not alone and the Lord is blessing and keeping me in his good time and pleasure. May the Lord keep me unto the end when all will be known.

*

Sun and sackcloth and earth shake – moon shakes the blood of sun and sackcloth and earth below. Sun scrolls the earth below and shakes. Mountains cover the kings and shake. All are shake. All are four that shake. It is the voice of shake – great mountain below the sun and blood of him who shakes four corners of sun. All must shake under the voice of sun and moon and kings – all behold how low the voice will hold and shake. Low the Earth and still the creatures and silence heaven and earth and below the earth. All are seven that are still until the trumpet shakes.

*

The island is very calm this morning, the air is cool, and my fish is fresh on the fire. I am thankful for the food and that the Lord has chosen to tell me of how the things after these things will be.

There will be woe, three measures of woe, the Lord has told me. Water will turn to flame and land will melt away. Blood will rain. When the trumpets of the Lord are blown the woe will be upon the powers of the earth. I am thankful for my food and that the Lord is keeping me from the woe to come for those who do not know that which is being made known will not repent. Blessed are those who hear and are chosen to hear.

*

It is a blessing to once again smell a burnt fish. As a young man I was called by the Lord out of a life in the sea to follow him and now he has brought me to this island to gaze and live on the sea. The Lord has made me a fisherman again in my old age. My last days will be like my first.

*

Lightning peals back the seals. Seal up lightning the covered seals. Make known the king the nations the prophet while lightning peals. Bitter stomach sealed. Peal it back. Lay low the sealed. Two ways to know last trumpet peals. Listen as the lightning falls and fells the seals. Witness the red two that peal. Measure the slain and the shaken seals. Sackcloth measured desirous peals. Measure the red the sealed. Make witness of war and measure felled and broken sealed. Torment who measure the seals. Shaking waste the two the red the witness the peals of death seal. Behold seven still trumpets silent two woes laid low. Hold the throne how long, you know how long.

*

The Lord has promised an end to the notes in the night. The Lord has promised me peace and companionship. The Lord now knows how hard it has been for his most Beloved on this island.

I have reminded the Lord of how much he loves me – of how he took me with him when he was to be Transfigured – of how I was the fastest runner of the twelve, the most receptive to his teachings, the one who took care of his mother when he left us, the one who recognized him as the Logos when no one else did. I slept on his shoulder at the last table. He remembers all of this now and all is well. All is known.

*

Today a woman and many beasts. Today is a day for wisdom and the wise. The Lord has promised me understanding and companionship, and this morning I see a woman walking the shore. She has thin arms and legs and a large stomach full of life. She is beautiful but also colored by blood. The Lord is being good to me. She is good for me. I will go and see.

*

The animals are in mutiny. Every beast of the island has left their minds behind. I do not know what to make of it and I have not seen the woman all afternoon. But there are leopards and eagles and wolves. All are running and none of them belong. I need to pray and seek. I have not sought the Lord and the island is in an uproar. This is all my doing. I hope to see the woman soon. But wait – flying things! I must seek.

*

I have told the Lord I will no longer sleep. He is good and just and true and I have not found any notes when I wake as he has promised. But I find other things – I find omens and beasts. I wake and smell the musk of lamb and lion, but I see no lamb or lion. I am unfit. I am thin and unfit. I am a prophet without a prophecy. I am patient. I am worn. I am John. I am alone. I am again. I am at an end.

*

I have not slept. The Lord knows this. I am going to make seven bowls – one for each day of the week – one for each day of not sleep. I have mud. I can use it to make the bowls. I have sun. I can use it to cook the made bowls.

*

It is time for the bowls to be dedicated. One is for pagan fools, one is for fish, one is for faith, one is for flames, one is for deeds, one is for drought, one is for the end of things. This is what the Lord had me do today. The meaning making of bowls. It is done.

*

The woman is drunk. She is wounded or vicious or what I do not know but she is covered in blood and she is dancing drunk. She is jumping mad. She is wonderful. I want to know her name and what she had killed or what beast has drew her blood. I want to taste her tongue. I want the blood on my face. I don't want the Lord to see any of this. I want to be naked in blood and covered in her wine. I want to taste. I want to be with again. I want to be with.

*

Babylon was destroyed before Jerusalem. The difference is Babylon will be destroyed again. But who will make it. Who will end it?

*

The island has song. It sings this to me – "hallelujah! Salvation and glory and power belong to the Lord because his judgments are true and righteous for he has judged the woman of corruption and he has avenged her blood. Her smoke rises up forever and ever. The twenty four elders and the four creatures fall down and worship the Lord and sing Amen hallelujah, and praise from small and great. Hallelujah for the Lord the Almighty the King." It sings incessantly. It sings to me. I sing to me. We sing for the King.

*

There is no deception left to be sung. The Lord is coming for me soon. There is one more war for me to lead. There is one more war for heaven and earth and below the earth to witness. The Lord will lead. The Lord has a sword to shake the nations with. The Lord is white. The Lord will make red the earth. I will be saved. I hear. Some will not hear. Many will be marked in red. But soon. I will be remade and taken back to Jerusalem and all will be made white and only red will be remade by the blood of unworthy kings. The Beloved will become a son.

*

There is light and the lamp is the lamb.

*

These words are faithful and true and blessed is he who heeds the prophecy of this book. And I, John, am the one who heard and saw these things. Do not seal up the words of the prophecy of this book for the time is near. The Lord is coming quickly to rend to men what they have done. It will be an end. Blessed are those whose gates are washed and dogs lay low. This is the prophecy of the Lord and cursed is the one who adds to this book. Yes, the Lord is coming quickly, and after these things we eat grace of meat and blood of grace.

———————————————

These are the words of my master – the words I must take. The fathers believe there is a great need presented here. The fathers believe the Lord is working in these words and that I must now make them into what the church needs to survive the wrath of Rome. If the end is coming soon, then come quickly, Lord. Lord come soon.

CPSIA information can be obtained
at www.ICGtesting.com
Printed in the USA
FSOW03n1645300816
24398FS